SLOCUM AND THE CHEROKEE MANHUNT

"I'm the law here, Klanghorn," Slocum said.

"I'd like you to tell me what you mean, Marshal." J. C. was holding his temper with difficulty.

"I mean this man here is not Hendry Chimes."

"How do you know that?"

"There weren't two Hendry Chimes at Lawrence. Only the one."

"That's what I just got through telling you," snapped Chimes.

"Then you're lying."

Klanghorn took a step between them, holding up his hands. "I want to know what you two men are fighting about. Slocum, why do you say he isn't what he says he is? That's what I want to know!"

"There was only one Hendry Chimes with Quantrill and it is not this man."

"How do you know that?"

"Chimes is dead."

"How do you know that?"

"I know because I killed him."

JAKE LOGAN

SLOCUM AND THE CHEROKEE MANHUNT

BERKLEY BOOKS, NEW YORK

SLOCUM AND THE CHEROKEE MANHUNT

A Berkley Book/published by arrangement with
the author

PRINTING HISTORY
Berkley edition/October 1987

ISBN: 0-425-10419-2

PRINTED IN THE UNITED STATES OF AMERICA

10 9 8 7 6 5 4 3 2 1

1

Rounding the low cutbank on the little dun pony, Slocum got his first look at the town. It lay on the prairie without much to tell where it began or ended in the tawny land. It too was brown, dusty, looking like something that had been dropped there. Like a lot of Western towns of that time and place; the Wyoming Territory of the eighties.

Slocum knew something about Horse Creek. It had a reputation, though not matching anything like Abilene, Deadwood, or Dodge. Some might have seen the place as just a raucous community at the fork where the trail to Denver split away from the wagon route to Oregon. A resting point for immigrants, buffalo hunters, and the U.S. Army caravans going to Nebraska, Colorado, and the Wyoming garrisons.

An effective number of gunfighters, buffalo skinners and wolfers, trail tramps, and other shadowy characters drifted in and out of Horse Creek. Men with summer names, itchy fingers, and a one-way view of life collected here in this town that Slocum had heard "made hell look real good."

Horse Creek was a place where a gunman could hang low for a spell, an in-between place where the busy gambler with too much light shining on him elsewhere could withdraw for a while, drop out of view until the climate took a change. In Horse Creek, questions were never asked; yet Slocum saw it as a place where a man could pick up news he couldn't find elsewhere. If he was shrewd and didn't mind taking risks. If he was patient and didn't sit with his back to a door.

He was turning this over in his mind as he rode toward the town with the noonday sun beating down on him from the cobalt sky, the heat shimmering up from the hard, bony trail. Funny—funny how one thing led to another. If he hadn't taken part in the war between the stock growers and the small cattlemen in Johnson County, he wouldn't have run afoul of the law; he wouldn't have run into Sheriff Clay Handy, and he wouldn't have been handed an ultimatum by that same peppery gentleman.

"You find Hagstrom for me, Slocum, and we'll drop the charges against you."

"You got a notion where he might be headed?"

"Nope." The sheriff of Big Horn was a man of few words, and he never repeated himself. It was said of him that he could chew more tobacco faster and spit less than any man west of the Mississippi.

As though giving the lie to this he spat now, co-piously, splattering the beaten cuspidor that was at the foot of his desk; and then he re-spat. He sniffed, reached to his pocket, and drew forth a plug of fresh tobacco and a clasp knife. "Cherokee Bill Hagstrom is about as not-known as a man can get. There ain't no picture of him, no flyer that's worth a damn by way of description—that I know—excepting he's big, strong as a bull, swift with a gun, and he don't value human life no more'n that." And Clay Handy had snapped his fingers like a pistol shot; then, holding the cut of chewing tobacco on the knife blade, he popped it into his mouth. "Hardly anyone—if maybe nobody at all, for the matter of that—has ever seen him face-to-face-like. Nobody knows what he looks like, least not a one who'll admit to it."

"I sure appreciate all the help you're giving me, Sheriff," Slocum said, and his face was as blank as a board when Clay Handy cut his eye quick at his prisoner, checking for hokum.

"I could press a charge on you, Slocum. No trouble. Getting people to riot, shooting at the law, etcetera, etcetera." He held up a big, flat, bony palm even though Slocum hadn't been about to defend himself. "I know. I know it. You was just helping them poor little cowmen going up against the big dishonest Cattle Growers Association." And suddenly his leathery face split into a big grin. "Exceptin' I am here to hold the law. You reading this with me, Slocum?" That grin suddenly changed to a slash in the wrinkled face.

"Every word," John Slocum said gravely, pious as a judge. "Just one thing: I don't go for bounty hunting."

Clay Handy squinted out of one eye then, and he'd even paused in his chewing. "Who said anything about bounty? You will be doing this for the law. You are working for me, for the government, and so you're like my deputy, exceptin' I am not pinning any tin on you. And I ain't paying you!"

"That's what I know," Slocum said, enjoying the way the sheriff delivered himself. "I'm mentioning the fact that there is a sizable bounty on Cherokee Bill."

"By private citizens. You figurin' on collecting same?"

"I am saying that there are a lot of people—other than the law—interested in locating Mr. Hagstrom, that's all I am saying." And he came down hard on these last words.

Clay Handy heard him. His tone was severe now as he said, "You bring Cherokee Bill in alive. I want the son of a bitch to stand trial."

"And if he doesn't want to come in alive?"

Sheriff Clay Handy scratched his belly just inside one of his wide yellow galluses, then settled back in his chair. "Then I reckon you got one alternative."

Slocum nodded. "Makes it easy, doesn't it."

Clay Handy glared at him He had big, shiny gray eyes that looked like painted glass. "You bring him in—hot or cold—but I want him mostly breathing."

Slocum knew he could have gotten away with it —simply vamoosed, GTT, Gone To Texas, as the saying had it. He'd skipped before when the atmosphere got too close. But he told himself he had nothing better to do, and since the sheriff had told him that Hagstrom was known to hang around Horse Creek and prey on the miners at the Crazy Woman diggings, he'd remembered that he'd always wanted to take a look at the place.

It was early afternoon when he rode into the dusty main street. The town was torpid, though not dead.

There was movement. Outside the Ajax Feed and Hardware, two box wagons waited while their drivers were inside getting their orders filled; a string of ponies stood at the hitch rail outside the Three Aces Saloon and Dance Hall kicking at flies, while there were a fair number of pedestrians stirring beneath the blistering sun; cowhands, miners, gambling folk, merchants, and even a few ladies. There was a rooming house, a barbershop and bath, some offices, five saloons; and there were various businesses— doctor, smithy, a livery, a carpenter shop, three eateries, a hotel, a bank, and an undertaker. There was also a newspaper. The guts of a town was here.

The Three Aces looked like a good place to start. Hard to tell from the outside; most saloons looked alike, and most were—trail whiskey, poor food, warm beer, the girls just serviceable at best.

Slocum dismounted and wrapped his reins loosely around the hitch rail; not tying them, keeping them loose so that if the horse spooked, he wouldn't snap the leather, and even more important, if the rider had to make a fast get-out-of-town, he wouldn't have to mess with untying anything.

Inside the Three Aces the light was dim. Slocum was thinking maybe that was just as well. A lot of saloons didn't bear clear scrutiny.

The man on the sober side of the bar seemed to pick right up on Slocum's thought. "Dark in here, ain't it?" He had an enormous belly and narrow shoulders. His fingers were long and tapering and kept twitching, moving about on the mahogany in spite of their owner.

Slocum nodded agreeably. "There are places that have too much light I know for a fact," he said.

The big man grunted; it came from down in his belly as he leaned against the bar and one of his shirt buttons popped. He paid no attention to it.

"Name it," he said.

"Whiskey."

The long jittery fingers reached down for a bottle.

"Your good stuff," Slocum said.

"It is all the same, mister."

"That why you got it so dark in here?"

Pouring, his eyes firmly on the glass, the bartender said, "Now, you wouldn't really want to see what's in that whiskey, would you?"

"Sorry I mentioned it," Slocum said, and he lifted his glass.

"Just drink it slow," the fat man said. "Let it eat its way to your boot soles."

For a few moments Slocum thought that was just what it was doing.

"Oren strains the tobacco leaves and snake heads outa that stuff every morning," said a voice down at the end of the bar.

And a string of mild laughter ran through some of the men near him.

Slocum smiled appreciatively, nodded at the man who had spoken, and took out a quirly and lit up. The bartender moved away, his hand hidden in the dank-smelling rag as he wiped the mahogany, breathing sterterously with his task.

Slocum was handling his whiskey slowly; he'd only ordered it as an excuse to be at the bar, wanting to get the flavor of the place, to establish himself in the town just a bit, and to feel his way to the question of Cherokee Bill Hagstrom.

"Ridin' through, are you?" The voice came from a man who had slipped close to his elbow.

"Horace!" another voice called to the man who had spoken.

Slocum saw the flush come into the first man's face, and it crossed his mind that he could be a little loose in his head. Hell, a man didn't ask such a question just like that in this country.

Suddenly he was aware of the silence. It was as though the room had stopped. He turned to take a look around. Two or three more men had entered since he had. There were about fifteen in the place. A game of cards had been going at one of the round wooden tables but had now stopped. Some men were getting to their feet; two, three were moving toward the swinging doors.

Even the big bartender, Oren, was staring at him, as though seeing him in a new way. There was some whispering going on among the group at the far end of the bar.

"What's going on with you men?" Slocum said, deciding he'd had enough mystery. "Somebody got a polecat up his ass?"

He was trying to see more clearly, but the room was too dim. The group at the end of the bar seemed to be all face.

"I said . . ."

"Sorry, mister." It was Oren, following his bar rag as it brought him to where Slocum was standing. "Sorry about it, mister."

"Sorry about what? What are you sorry about?" He wanted to see their faces, but it was hard with the room so poorly lighted. The saloon was now absolutely still. The only sound came from the fat bartender's wet breathing.

This strange tableau was accentuated when the swinging doors burst open and a man walked in and stopped abruptly, pulling himself into an immediate, guarded attention. He was evidently one of the townsmen, not a cowhand or miner, for he was wearing a frock coat; an older man with long white hair.

"I said, what's the matter?" Slocum snapped, beginning to let his anger show.

The new arrival had stared at him with a look of incredulity on his face. And for a moment Slocum just watched him, returning his look, studying him. The man must have been at least seventy. He gave Slocum the impression of a Mississippi riverboat gambler. He was dressed nattily and he carried a cane. His eyes were bright, quick, and intent. Suddenly he seemed to come to a decision, and he swept the top hat from his head.

"I must ask your pardon, sir—we..." And his eyes swept the group at the end of the bar. "We—uh —I believe we may have mistaken you for another— uh—for someone else." He paused to cough mildly into his pale fist, though this was more of a theatrical gesture than a need, Slocum could see.

"And who did you think I was?" Slocum asked, his irritation giving way completely to alertness, while his hand moved imperceptibly toward the Colt .45 rigged for cross draw. He was aware that the men at the end of the bar hadn't moved, nor had Oren the bartender. Checking the mirror on one of the sidewalls, he knew there was nobody behind him.

"I believe we thought you were somebody and—

uh—I think we're still not sure." This was followed by the old man throwing his eyes in the direction of the silent group and Oren and, receiving no support there, returning to Slocum with a little smile. "I, for one, sir, don't believe you are who we thought you were."

"Are you going to tell me who?"

"We mistook you for a gentleman named—uh—Hagstrom."

"Cherokee Bill. I see."

The other man nodded, advancing to the bar now. "Quite. Yes, indeed. I am glad you understand, sir. Allow me to introduce myself. Colonel Humboldt Smithers, formerly a commissioned officer in the Army of the Confederacy, presently editor, publisher, and owner of the *Horse Creek Gazette*—we publish bi-weekly—and also . . . and also doctor of medicine, though mostly retired from that profession, since we have a good man in practice—good, more or less. I'd amend that to 'adequate,' but the boy is learning. For myself, I help out when and if there is an emergency. For the most part . . ." He paused, smiling now, taking his glass, which the bartender had placed before him. "Mostly I observe life. At three score and ten I have finally accepted to become my true self; an incorrigible observer of *Homo sapiens*." He signaled to Oren to refill Slocum's glass. Then he raised his own in a toast and drank.

"I am so glad you're not Cherokee Bill Hagstrom."

"So am I," Slocum said.

"You see, no one here knows what he looks like."

"But what if I had been Cherokee Bill? What, then?"

The Colonel lowered his glass. "Why, then, sir. Why, then . . ." His eyes had strayed to a girl who was descending the stairs that led to the balcony and bedrooms above. But he came back to Slocum after registering some sort of opinion that was obviously sexual. "Why, then, sir, we would have been up shit creek." And he stood there wagging his white head dolefully.

Slocum had kept part of his attention in the mirror behind the bar so that he could see the girl. She had reached the floor now and was moving toward the other end of the room where he saw a door. He watched her go through it.

"That's—uh—one of our truly attractive young ladies," said the Colonel. "And let me add that our girls are definitely not without high quality—in character *and* in sexual prowess." He cocked his head at his companion. Slocum was aware that the men in the room had fallen back into conversation, though maintaining a guarded, somber mood.

"May I know your name, sir?" the Colonel asked carefully, still regarding him with his head tilted to one side.

"I'm John Slocum."

The bushy eyebrows shot up. "Indeed! John Slocum! And that is a surprise infinitely more acceptable than had you been Cherokee Bill Hagstrom!"

"But I'm asking you, what if I had been? You say you'd have been up shit creck, but what does that mean? What did you expect from Cherokee Bill?"

Slocum had lowered his voice so that the others would not hear him asking his question this time. He felt there was a good deal more in what Humboldt Smithers had said than his words. The atmosphere of the room alone indicated there was something heavy engaging the whole town.

The Colonel cleared his throat slowly and now lowered his voice even more as he said, "What did we expect, you ask? We have been expecting him to come in here and kill us all; that is what we've been expecting, sir!"

"All of you?" Slocum stared at his companion.

"Those of us—and I am not one, I hope—whom he considers run the town; and, uh, who were in on the unfortunate action last week." Colonel Humboldt Smithers moved closer to Slocum, almost touching him. Slocum noticed that he smelled of tobacco and onion. "I realize you are ignorant of what took place. I refer to the action, sir, where a half dozen or so of our good citizens—and do not ask me for names!—decided to engage in a lynching."

"Who did they lynch?"

"They lynched Cherokee Bill's younger brother."

2

In a back room of another saloon in town, four men sat around a table. This was a room without windows, and the two coal-oil lamps that lighted the premises threw shadows against the wall, and sometimes up onto the low ceiling. A fifth man had just entered. He was tall, gristly, in his sixties, with a long nose and deep-socketed eyes. The four at the table turned their attention fully upon him.

But the new arrival was already shaking his head. "No news," he said. "Nothing."

A sigh seemed to pass through everyone at the table as the man who had spoken took the chair that had obviously been waiting for him.

"Well, Clem?" These words came from a heavy man wearing a clean brown Stetson hat with a crisp, straight brim.

Clem Dunstan sat down heavily and accepted the drink that someone poured for him. "Boys, we are in a tight."

All looked even more somber at these words.

The man in the brown Stetson reached to the

pocket that spread tightly across almost half of his big chest and withdrew a cigar. "You're not helping us, Clem. I'd allow we know that already."

"But what can we do?" said a thickly bearded man as he drummed his fingers on the table. "What in the hell can we do? Just sit here like a bunch of prairie chickens waiting to be shot to hell?"

"Or—heaven?" said Parker Tilbury, speaking around his fresh Havana as he lighted it with a flaming lucifer.

"Parker, I don't believe that is funny. This is no time for such a talk." These scolding words fell from the thick lips of Tod Ollenburgh, the town lawyer; a man with shoulders hunched with importance.

"No offense, Tod. But there's no sense in our getting into a bind over it. Hell, we made a mistake. So we'll see how to fix it." Parker Tilbury was like his hat: crisp, clean, neat, and hard-brimmed. A man in his fifties, he owned the Ajax Feed and Hardware.

John Bettman scratched into his heavy beard, as with his other hand he reached for the bottle in front of him. "Boys, another round." And without waiting for a response, he poured, the wings of his hairy nose tightening somehow from the effort. The group was silent until the ritual was completed.

All drank, their faces serious with the gravity of the situation which they, as some of the town's leading citizens and members of the council, now faced.

The only one of the five who had not spoken was a gloomy man dressed all in black, with black hair combed tightly down on top of his bony head, and with long black sideburns. He spoke now.

"Gentlemen, we are in a tight, as indeed our colleague, Mr. Dunstan, has pointed out so clearly."

The raspy, sarcastic tone came out of thin, tight lips. An unnecessary addition to the conversation, some of those present might have supposed; except that Ed Deal, the town's banker and mayor, never said anything without a reason. And as it developed, Deal, who happened also to be the town's sole undertaker, was only warming the group into what he really had to say.

"Boys, gentlemen, I feel that we've given enough time to the problem of Mr. Hagstrom. My hands are clean—and so are yours. Well—" His glance moved slowly around the table, pausing briefly at each face and passing on. "The man— the murderer and rapist—was brought to swift and honest justice. As far as I am concerned, the episode is closed." As someone started to speak, he held up his hand. "There's no point going into it any further. Yes, we acted as vigilantes without benefit of the law. But what law? Our town marshal is now residing in the cemetery, and no replacement has been sent. What were we to do? Let the killer and molester go free? Don't even ask such a stupid question! No—the episode is closed. And what we can do now is remain silent. I mean—silent! Only we in this room know who was there."

"Unfortunately some others in town have heard about Dummy Jensen's brother," said Clem Dunstan. "Hell, nobody even knew he had a brother."

"Or anything else," Parker Tilbury added, "since that boy was crazy as a loon."

Tod Ollenburgh placed his hands flat on the table and leaned forward, making his point. "I'm of a mind with Ed. Let's drop it. Nothing's going to happen; and if there are elements in town want to spread gossip and lies, let 'em. They weren't there, and they don't know who was!"

"I'm with that," snapped John Bettman, scratching his beard in emphasis of what he was saying.

Ed Deal lifted his glass. "Good, then. Now we can get down to the real business at hand."

The winter had been a tough one, and spring had come to the country late. But now it was summer and the land was greening.

John Slocum heard it in the streets of the little town. Horse Creek was rife with a double expectancy—on the one hand the apprehension, and even downright fear, that was spreading over the possible visitation of Cherokee Bill Hagstrom, who would wreak massive vengeance for the lynching of Dummy Jensen, his beloved brother. His *kid* brother, to boot. This was emphasized among the gossipers; that because Dummy was the younger, then Cherokee would be even more angry. Of course, nobody knew for certain if the famous outlaw, desperado, killer—who once set a ten-year-old boy to a bullet dance for spooking his horse—had yet heard the news. But bad news, especially when people try to suppress it, travels with utmost speed.

And on the other hand, and in a quite different key, the town was wringing with excitement over the expected arrival of the first Texas trail herd. Horse Creek was about to become a shipping point for Texas cattle.

Slocum felt the excitement growing even as the sun began to go down, its dying light reaching gently across the grubby little town, touching the wooden buildings, the dirt streets, the brand-new cattle pens down at the just completed railhead. As evening deepened, lamps were lighted and the current of expectancy grew.

Funny, he reflected, how sometimes events came in mixed bundles—the big excitement of the cattle drive with all the business and difficulties it would bring to the little town, which was already too small; and the grim, gray apprehension of the long shadow of Cherokee Bill Hagstrom bent on vengeance—the killer whose identity nobody was at all sure about, and so he could stalk his victim with impunity. And he would.

Yet, as Humboldt Smithers had pointed out to Slocum, the only ones really to feel legitimately guilty would be the lynch mob. But where there is fear, which might be well earned by those who are the guilty ones, the same fear can be shared by the innocent, as though they who had no hand in whatever was committed, yet supported it somehow with their feelings of apprehension, their private thrill; sucking their anguish even though they had had nothing whatever to do with the miserable deed that had engendered the state of fear. Fear being always catching in the way of an epidemic.

Slocum and the Colonel had walked over to the office of the *Horse Creek Gazette,* there to partake of some special strong spirits the springy old man had offered. Humboldt was bubbling with gossip, news, trivia, and anecdote.

"To my mind, sir, there is only one way to handle this Cherokee Bill fellah." The Colonel's voice was even more heavily Southern under the persuasion of alcohol. He looked at Slocum, his white eyebrows lifted high, pushing up the deep wrinkles on his forehead, his china-blue eyes glistening like rinsed marbles. "See, Slocum—do ya?—the men in Hoss Creek just ain't men. I mean, in the real sense of the word, the way myself and yourself know it."

"How so?" Slocum asked genially, enjoying the moment with Humboldt Smithers. The old boy had the energy of ten. "You mean, they got no guts?"

"That is correct, sir. That is precisely what I am saying." He lowered his voice, even though they were alone. "Damn Yankees is what the trouble is."

Slocum grinned.

The Colonel swept on. "You know, Lead City, Colorado, do you?" He cocked his head but grew impatient when Slocum didn't answer right away. "Well, it don't matter whether you do or you don't. I want to just tell you about this feller Cherokee Bill— back some years ago . . . and a man, a real man . . . General Mordecai Jason Winton. Just a little bit of history to let you know what sort of man Hagstrom is. I mean—he's a vicious killer!"

"I know that, Colonel. What I need to know about is the doings right now here in Horse Creek." Slocum said, quickly cutting him off. "I've been hoping you could fill me in on just what's been happening around here. I mean, with the lynching and all that, and this feller, Cherokee. Hell, you know those men in the Three Aces they like to took me for himself. Now, wouldn't that've been a helluva note!"

The Colonel's rich chuckle was already rolling down his long, lean chest even before Slocum finished speaking. "Indeed! Indeed it would, sir! If they'd had the guts of a pair of piss ants, they'd have strung you up right then and there and no more ado about it. Only, like I was just trying to tell you, they—"

"Tell me what happened," Slocum said. "I heard they had a lynching. Tell who, what, where, when, how, and how come?"

Again the chuckling took over Humboldt Smithers's spare, but always eager, body. "I reckon I better tell you, young feller. Let's see now. Matter of fact—well, no. No, that wouldn't do."

Slocum waited with immense patience while the old man backed and filled, then suddenly burst out with, "The assholes! The veritable assholes! Let me tell you, Slocum, I could write *some story* for the *Gazette*. You could bet your balls on it! I wasn't there, mind you. But I know who was." And he lowered his voice again, this time almost to a whisper, throwing his eyes cautiously to the door, the window. "There, there. I better shut my mouth."

But Slocum knew that was impossible. "It'll go no further," he promised. "But I need to know what's going on. I've got to survive, too, you know."

Humboldt appreciated the sly comment. He was like a dammed-up Niagara chomping to be released. "You know, you got to keep this to yourself. I could get myself shot for what I know—and what I *surmise,* sir. What I *surmise!* Don't never let it be said that Humboldt Smithers doesn't know how to put two and two together!"

"Why not just tell me what you know."

"There was the young feller Dummy Jensen. Well, no, let me start again. There was this girl—ah, yes. A real sweet young girl. *Norah.* Norah Kenton. And she was out walking with her boyfriend one evening. Some said he was her fiancé—just about getting to be, anyways. Johnnie Hoad. Carpenter's apprentice, John was. Nice-looking lad. Well, they was found the next day about a mile out of town where they'd gone walking. Johnnie with his head split open. And Norah some distance away—strangled, raped."

The Colonel paused, his eyes staring, reliving the scene as though he'd actually been through it himself somehow when the bodies were discovered.

"I was in the Double Dice when the men came in after. Sitting there near them. They was that intent, they didn't see me. Not that it matters. Anyhow, they were all thrown—I mean *thrown*—by what they'd found. They'd all come back from the posse that rode out. And they'd found nobody. Was it a soldier? One of them buffalo skinners? A wolfer? Whoever it was, everybody they questioned had an answer— and a witness, to boot."

He coughed suddenly, spat, scratched himself vigorously between the legs, and resumed swiftly. "Armed men and boys roamed the streets of Horse Creek, and they were nobody to mess with. The town was in a big temper. Norah had been well liked in town. And Johnnie Hoad, too; but especially the girl. And I heard later that when Norah's body was found—it was her father Tom Kenton found her— and he swore by God he was going to get the son of a bitch and—you can guess what!"

"Excepting they didn't find anybody," Slocum said, filling in as Humboldt Smithers paused briefly.

"Excepting they found nothing. Then . . ." He held up his hand dramatically, lowering his voice again. "Then somebody—yes, it was Henry Brobick, a rancher—asked them right there in the bar if anybody'd figured, like he was figurin', that it was likely no stranger that did the deed. Well, this took the wind out of them for a minute. And Henry went on to ask had anyone thought of Dummy Jensen, the deaf and dumb boy who did odd jobs around town. And he reminded everybody how about a year back, Dummy had beaten a drunken horse wrangler to near death because said horse wrangler had made a dirty gesture when Norah walked by."

Humboldt stopped, reached for his glass for support, and swallowed liberally, coughing, almost gagging, slapping his chest with his bony fist and then straightening a little, wheezing, coughing out a round of laughter at his helplessness. "Age, sir. Age. Seventy winters in this great world of adventure and the signs are beginning to show. In the corners, sir! Hah! Where was I?"

"You were telling me how the crowd in the bar began to whip themselves into a lynch party, I believe," Slocum said calmly.

"Sure enough, that's what they did! Bill Wellman, who runs the Bonus Eatery, he pointed out that Dummy defended Norah that time with the horse wrangler on account of she was one of the few people in this town who didn't make fun of him and told them that by God, that didn't prove he raped and killed her!

"And then, on top of that, right then, Jock Kramer, the livery hostler, told how at the time Norah must have been attacked, Dummy was helping him rub down a couple of horses; right in town, at the livery!"

"But they didn't believe it," Slocum said.

"They didn't believe it." Humboldt almost sighed

the words. He wagged his head slowly, staring into the scene that had taken place so recently in the Double Dice Saloon.

"Then what?" Slocum prompted.

The Colonel's pointed shoulders rose in an elaborate shrug. "They just didn't hear those men defending Dummy Jensen. They started to pile out of the saloon."

"Liquored."

"You can bet on it. Plenty couraged up with the booze. The pieces I got fit a picture: They caught Dummy down by the livery and strung him up on a cottonwood. They botched it. They didn't tie the rope right because they were in a hurry likely, and he fell. Then they hadn't thought to tie his feet, so he started to run. He was deaf and dumb, remember, and so he couldn't understand what they were doing to him. He couldn't even holler! Christ, they made a mess of it! He ran a ways with his hands tied behind his back, and they caught him and strung him up again. The second time they did it; they hanged him." Humboldt lifted his glass slowly, apparently stunned himself merely by recounting his story. Then he seemed to shake himself, ran the palm of his hand over his face, sniffed, belched. "Gutless scum! But let me get on with my story about Cherokee as a young man—a boy, really—and old General Mordecai Winton. Why, the general was the only man in that damn Colorado town who had the guts of a man, let me tell you! Not like Hoss Creek! I was there, I saw it all. Lead City was a quiet, God-fearing town of law-abiding citizens. Then this fellow Cherokee rode in. Just a kid he was. But he was wearing a brace of mean-looking pistols.

"He'd rode in on a Sunday—you know what a Sunday afternoon is in a town like that. It ain't Sunday—it is the Holy Sabbath! Anyway, a while later, down the street comes a shabby old mutt dog; Clyde his name was. He was sort of known to everybody in town. He came down the street with a couple of big tin cans tied to his tail, and he is followed by this, like, sixteen-year-old kid wearing a great big Stetson hat, bat-wing chaps, and carrying a brace of six-guns."

"Cherokee . . ." Slocum put in.

The Colonel nodded. "The old dog Clyde just made it to the general's door—they were friends, the general used to feed him—and dropped in his tracks, whether more from fright or exhaustion, take your pick. Anyway, the general heard the commotion and came out. Hobbling. See, he'd been shot up badly at Manassas. He starts waving his arms and shouting, 'Stop that, you scoundrel! Leave that dumb brute in peace!'

"'Sure, Pop,' says Cherokee, obliging as all hell, mind you; and he whips up his two six-guns and shoots Clyde right in the head. 'There!,' he says, 'I done what you said—left him in peace.' And he collapses with laughter!"

The Colonel paused for further liquid support and leaned back in his chair.

"I have heard of Cherokee's kind of humor," Slocum said wryly.

Humboldt took another drink. "The general didn't bat an eye. He told that damn hooligan to wait there. Then he went into the house and came back out almost immediately. He was carrying an old Confederate rifle. 'You shot Clyde, you son of a bitch,' he says. And he lifted the rifle, and Cherokee shot him right between the eyes." The Colonel paused. "See, the general was an old man; some people thought he was a hundred. The rifle wasn't loaded."

"The old man had guts," Slocum said. "I see what you mean." Slocum had been listening patiently to this endless story from the Colonel's past, but he could no longer contain himself. "Colonel, I know Hagstrom's record—enough, anyway. So let's get back to the lynching. What happened afterwards?"

Humboldt gave a start. Clearly he'd been miles away—with General Mordecai Winton, Clyde the faithful dog, and Cherokee's quaint sense of humor. He rallied. He took a stiff pull at his drink and leered at his visitor; the proprietor of superior knowledge.

"Sir, you are the most impatient Southerner I have ever yet met. But I like you—I like you," he added swiftly, holding up a restraining palm. "Now let me see, where were we?"

"You were telling about the lynch mob. They'd just strung Dummy to the cottonwood for the second time."

"Ah, yes, yes . . ." He cleared his throat. "Somebody—I believe I'd heard it was, well, I don't rightly recollect the name—someone went through the dead man's pockets. Hell, the body had to be buried. Undertaking job. An indigent youth, so the council would have to shell out six, seven dollars for burial. So someone went through his pockets to see if he had money, and by God, they were sure sorry they did." A report like a toy cannon popped out of the Colonel's round mouth, which Slocum accepted as a laugh of astonishment. "Yes, yes—the man searching those pockets found no money, but he came up with a letter. A letter that turned everybody into the shakes, I can sure imagine. I can see them now. . . . You know who that letter was from?"

"Cherokee Bill."

"Dummy's big brother! Phew!" He whipped his gray head around two, three times, whistling with amazement and awe.

"You know Cherokee Bill?" Slocum asked. "Have you ever seen him?"

"I don't count the gentleman amongst my close or even distant acquaintances, sir. In point of fact, I have not seen him since he was that sixteen-year-old brat in Lead City." He suddenly whipped out a huge red bandanna and wiped his nose vigorously, blew loudly, wiped again, and returned the bandanna to his hip pocket.

Slocum was impressed; the old man had drawn that bandanna with the speed and expertise of a gunfighter.

"I'll give you a brief rundown on Cherokee Bill Hagstrom," the Colonel said. "People here are scared shitless of him. And not without reason. He's a bank robber, stage robber, and a horse and cattle rustler. These, as you know, are not uncommon occupations in this time and place, but Cherokee is not your run-of-the-mill desperado. As my recent tale has already revealed to you, he is as vindictive, as vicious and unscrupulous as any fiend. He has ambushed posses with a shotgun, he has hanged men by their ankles— alive, leaving them to die at the end of the rope. He has tortured men, shot women and children. And the Lord knows what else."

"Well, you're right about one thing," said Slocum.

"And that is . . . ?"

"Cherokee will sure as hell be paying Horse Creek a visit."

"Exactly, sir!" The Colonel swept to his feet. "Precisely! And by now he's very possibly heard the news. He will pause only for the length of time it takes him to plan the most hideous revenge. You can be sure of that! God, what a time for this to happen!"

"Because of the cattle drive and the railroad," Slocum said.

"Precisely so! It couldn't have happened at a worse time. Just when the town is starting to move, to grow, those idiots go and foul everything."

"It's going to be as bad for the innocent as for the guilty ones, Colonel," Slocum said thoughtfully.

"How so?" The Colonel's mouth had turned into a perfect O, and he raised his eyebrows almost to his hairline.

"Like how's a citizen going to know when Cherokee will be around?"

"But not everyone," said the Colonel. "Not everybody will have that concern. Only those guilty of the crime."

"You don't get my point, Colonel. A man like Cherokee Bill isn't going to worry about the finer honesties and judgments, the niceties of who's guilty and who isn't."

"You mean . . . ?" Humboldt Smithers's face had turned the color of ash.

"I mean, Cherokee Bill will be measuring the whole town, my friend."

"Everybody?"

"Everybody. That includes you."

"Good God! That man must be crazy, mad!"

"And remember, Colonel, everything you've ever heard about Cherokee Bill Hagstrom is true. Plus one more thing."

"What would that be?" The Colonel sat down carefully, as though he were afraid of falling in the face of what new thing Slocum was going to bring.

"He is, above all else, effective."

"I know that, young man."

"No, you don't," Slocum said. "You only know the stories. Cherokee rode with Bill Anderson during the war."

"Bloody Bill, you mean?" Humboldt's eyes were popping. "You mean Quantrill's lieutenant!"

Slocum nodded.

"You—you knew him?"

"Never laid eyes on him—Hagstrom, you mean."

"Jesus . . ." said the Colonel.

"I believe Hagstrom was at Centralia when Bloody Bill lined up those twenty-six soldiers and shot 'em in cold blood."

"Holy Mother of God!"

"I didn't know you were a man of the church, Colonel."

"I am now."

3

Slocum couldn't help but feel there was something missing in the puzzle. Somehow he just didn't feel it was all as cut-and-dried as Humboldt Smithers supposed it to be—and maybe the lynchers, too, for that matter. Sure, Cherokee could pick them off one by one or come into town one night and blast the lot of them. The guilty ones. But how would he find out who was in the actual lynching party? Would he really just go about murdering the citizens of the town indiscriminately? That would take a lot of doing. Not that Hagstrom was a man of scruples, but it would be inefficient, not really in keeping with his character as Slocum had discerned it. There was something too pat about him riding into Horse Creek and blasting away just like that. What little Slocum knew about Cherokee told him that at the very least the man was anything but a dumbbell. He didn't know exactly why, but he kept remembering something he'd heard about the man, which was his strange, macabre sense of humor. The story Humboldt Smithers had told him about Cherokee putting

27

the dog out of its misery, and another story he'd heard where Cherokee had asked a town marshal where he was from and the man had said, "Right here."

"I think we'll have to prove that," Cherokee was said to have replied. "Let's make you a permanent resident of this here place so's you won't ever have to move again." And he drew his six-gun and did just that.

Somehow those two stories fit a pattern, the pattern of a man who would go for the theatrics, a man who wouldn't do anything in just the simple, ordinary way.

It was late afternoon when Slocum walked into the Three Aces and ordered a drink. Fat Oren was on duty, and he grunted as he placed the bottle on the bar. "See you got through the day all right, mister."

"Didn't you expect me to?"

"Not so easy when you like come into town and get taken for a man the likes of Cherokee Bill Hagstrom."

"It was close," Slocum said, his eyes smiling in the corners as he watched the big bartender. He felt something coming.

The big man was sweating as he pushed the bar rag closer to where Slocum had put down his glass. "Somebody wants to see you," he said, keeping his eyes down, talking through tight lips, the bar rag not stopping. He lifted the glass, wiped beneath it. "The back room off to my right. Ease over there in a minute. Wait'll I'm at the other end of the bar."

Slocum studied his glass, not looking at the other man, apparently just savoring his drink, turning things over in his mind, like any cow waddy or traveler passing through. He waited till the barman was down at the other end of the long mahogany and then casually turned, leaning back with his elbows on the bar.

Just at that moment he saw the girl coming down the stairs that led to the balcony and rooms where the clientele, as Humboldt Smithers had put it, "could pleasure themselves." It was the same girl he'd seen when he was last here with the Colonel. At that time she'd given him a brief glance, and he'd known then that she was taking note of him as a potential; but this time her eyes felt him, and there was the trace of a smile on her face.

Slocum grinned at her. "Hello," he said. "What can I call you?"

She was blond, small, but with a very firm bust. He could see the staunch outline of her thighs in her silk dress. And he felt his loins stir most agreeably.

He heard Oren the bartender clear his throat behind him as the girl approached.

"My name's Wendy," she said.

"What would you like for a drink?" He turned and faced the scowl on Oren's face. The barman moved his big head slightly toward the door at the back of the room.

"I heard you," Slocum said agreeably. "Now be a nice fellow and give the lady a drink. What'll it be, honey?"

"Wendy get out of here," the fat man said to the girl, and his jowls had stopped quivering. He looked like a furious bull.

"Mister, I told you to get the lady a drink." Slocum's words fell like pieces of ice on the big bar.

Oren's lips started to move. In the next instant,

with the bartender's next sentence not even started, Slocum had reached across the bar and grabbed him by the collar. "I said . . . get that drink!"

For a split second the revolt burned in Oren's pale eyes, but he was no match for the green ice he saw in his customer's look. He nodded, his breath coming fast, and stepped back from the bar. Slocum was watching him, his right hand close to his holstered six-gun.

A dead silence had fallen in the room. The Wheel of Fortune had stopped, conversation had died. From somewhere came the sound of a ticking clock, the guttering of somebody's pipe. Slocum was watching the room behind him in the mirror.

"Mister, maybe another time," the girl said.

He could feel her fear like she was gripping him with it.

"Nothing to be afraid of, young lady. In fact, I think now is good a time as any to establish relations with the people in this saloon." He had kept his eyes on the bartender the whole time he was speaking. "We'll have that drink now; and I do mean right now!"

Slocum could see the bulge in back of the fat man's neck redden as he turned to reach for the bottle.

Out of the corner of his eye, off to the bartender's right, Slocum saw the door to the back room open. He had stepped away from the bar so that he would be free for a fast draw if necessary. To his astonishment it was a woman who appeared, but a woman the likes of which he hadn't seen very often. She was young, dark, tall, beautiful. She was surely no hooker, and clearly sharp enough to size the situation immediately.

"Oren, give him what he wants. And—uh—Wendy, the same." And she stood there measuring him with her glance. He watched her carefully while he was also keeping his attention on the whole room. At the same time he was aware of his organ pressing like a club against his trousers. She stood very straight but also relaxed. Her bare arms were ivory smooth, and he could see the bulge of a pair of copious young breasts.

"At your convenience, Mister Slocum," she said then, her voice soft, firm, and coming from far back in her throat. She turned, and he watched the quiver of her buttocks as she walked back through the still-open door. And closed it quietly behind her.

The bartender was gripping the neck of the bottle hard as he poured.

"Relax," Slocum said pleasantly. "It's all in the day's work."

Oren said nothing.

"Who is that?" Slocum asked.

"That is Lady Godiva. She owns this here place. "God damn, I told you she wanted to see you."

"I heard you."

"Mister, it is no longer my business, but if I was you, I'd take another look-see. That lady is no person to mess with."

Slocum put down his glass. "And neither am I." He turned to the girl, who was still silent. "Let's move to a table, honey. Three's a crowd." And by holding his eyes on her and grinning broadly, he teased a smile out of her.

Even faced with the lush little creature who had

joined him for a drink, Slocum found his thoughts straying—just for a moment—to the lady in the doorway. Lady Godiva. Boy! She had balls or brass; or something. So, by God, let her wait. He was having a damn good time with his present companion, and it didn't take much—a certain look in her hazel eyes, the tip of her tongue poking between her full lips—for his erection to drive any thought of anyone else out of his mind. And out of his trousers.

By now Wendy had relaxed and, like himself, obviously had only one thought on her mind.

The saloon had returned to normal; and so, it seemed, had Oren. He even brought over a free drink. It didn't take Slocum much to realize he was into something with Lady Godiva. But—first things first, he told himself.

And he found himself pleasantly surprised—if not astonished—at the shapely beauty that undressed shortly in her upstairs room.

She was out of her clothes in a moment and, stepping toward him, straddled his erect cock. He started to hum in her ear as he danced her toward the bed. And in a moment he had her down on her back and had plunged deep into her soaking bush, driving firmly right up into he didn't know where. All the way up to her throat, maybe. She had opened herself completely as he rode her high and deep, murmuring with the joy that swept through her, while he felt his skin quivering all over him, from head to feet. Instinctively she matched his rhythm as he pumped, and their loins danced together now, more quickly but never hurried. She matched his strokes perfectly, playing her fingers along his back, down the crack of his buttocks, to his balls. He felt his load was going

to be extra big. And it was. She gasped and surged as
he came and came, filling her, their come spilling out
of her bush and down their thighs.

"Oh, I loved it," she said as he lay supine on top
of her. And something in her voice caught him. He
suddenly realized how small she was, and how gentle.

Later, as they lay side by side, she said, "Don't
forget your appointment."

"My appointment?"

"I'm sorry, I know it's none of my business, but I
know Godiva wants to see you."

"I think we need seconds," Slocum said, and his
hand reached down to her thick bush.

"I think so too."

"Gentlemen, the J.C. herd left the Canadian River a
month ago. Figuring on ten, twelve miles a day with
a herd that size, and the crew Klanghorn has, it'll
take thirty-five to forty days to get them here." It was
Ed Deal speaking, and the council listening.

"How many head is it?" someone asked.

"Burt said twenty-five hundred." Deal leaned forward and placed his elbow carefully on the green
baize cover.

"You can figure it out," he said.

"Any day now." Parker Tilbury shifted the crisp
brown Stetson hat on his closely cropped head.

"Exactly." Ed Deal lifted his elbow and leaned
back in his chair, his thin eyes measuring the four
men sitting around the table.

John Bettman cleared his throat, spat quickly. "It
isn't going to be easy," he said.

"You mean, like Dodge."

"If we don't learn something from what happened to Dodge, Newton, Abilene, Ellsworth, Wichita . . ." Clem Dunstan, having ticked the towns off on his fingers, let the sentence hang over the table, as he looked around at his colleagues.

Ed Deal leaned back in his chair, sniffing, clearing his throat. He had a lot of phlegm most of the time, or, as he referred to it himself, "catarrh."

Tod Ollenburgh was sitting next to him, now relighting his cigar, admiring it as he held it away after taking his first puffs, then returning it to his mouth. With the little finger of his left hand he reached into his ear and scratched vigorously. "I have a feeling we're all pointing in the same direction," he said, his voice rasping into the silence that had suddenly dropped onto the group.

"Well, then, why don't we get to that point," said Ed Deal. He had been waiting for just this moment. "The point is," he went on, not waiting for anyone to answer, "the point is we need a lawman. We've spoken of this before. We've got to appoint somebody."

Around the table heads nodded, and there was a murmur of agreement.

"But who?" Clem Dunstan brought the question that was in everyone's mind. "Who? Hell, we all know what a cattle town's like. You don't want anybody less than a gunfighter is how I see it."

"Ed, do you have anybody in mind?" It was Tod Ollenburgh speaking. He kept his eyes on Deal as he spoke, watching the banker as he received the question.

Deal was looking down at his hands, playing for the moment. "I believe I do," he said. "But—but there's still another matter to which we need to address ourselves, especially when we consider who would be the new marshal of Horse Creek."

Silence fell again, but it was a different one, for everyone's thoughts were now firmly, albeit unwillingly, on the same subject.

At last Parker Tilbury said it. "Cherokee Bill Hagstrom."

"Precisely." And Ed Deal's reply was said with all the precision that was needed to bring home to the group the wretched situation they were in. "We need a man who can handle *that* situation."

"Somebody who will understand we were simply executing the law," put in John Bettman.

"You have someone, Ed?" Ollenburgh asked again.

"I do," Deal replied, allowing a moment before he spoke. "I do have someone in mind. But we have to go carefully. I want to check a few things out before bringing up his name." He pushed his chair back, placed both hands on the edge of the table, and stood up.

The meeting was ended.

When Slocum came downstairs into the main bar, he found Oren the huge bartender waiting for him. Indeed, as he came down from Wendy's room, he felt the inquisitive eyes of the saloon on him. The atmosphere had changed visibly during his sojourn upstairs with the girl. It was electric, and he could feel it on the back of his neck, on his wrists, in his belly.

"Boss is expecting you," Oren said as he stepped to the bar. This time the tone was respectful, bordering on the tentative.

Slocum nodded.

"That door." The big man threw his eyes in the direction of the back room.

He was deciding whether to knock or just walk in, when all at once, the door opened and a man walked out. Seeing Slocum, he didn't close the door but left it open behind him, nodding just slightly as they passed each other.

"Do come in," the silky voice said as he crossed the threshold. "And please shut the door. And if you don't mind, make yourself at home. We'll wait just a moment. I've sent Harold for our drinks."

She was sitting on a horsehair sofa at one end of the room, over which some colorful rugs had been thrown. The floor was covered with rugs, and the entire room was impressive with the quality of decoration. Slocum had visited most of the lush spots in Denver and K.C. and Frisco, among others, and wasn't easily impressed. But he saw quickly that the lady in question—and there was no question in his mind that this was her taste—had traveled and could even be well educated. Her voice, which slipped so easily past her full, sensuous lips, seemed to fit right into the atmosphere of her quarters; and Slocum wondered if there were other rooms attached to this one. Or did the lady also have rooms elsewhere? It didn't matter, he decided, as Harold returned with a tray of glasses and bottles and some kind of appetizer food—crackers and cheese, it looked like.

"Mr. Slocum, will you do the honors? I'd like a strong one if you please. Oh, and"—she reached toward the small table in front of the sofa and opened a silver box—"may I offer you an extremely fine Havana? Only just shipped in from San Francisco."

Slocum had removed his hat and now smiled hap-

pily as the odor of that good tobacco entered the
room. The cigar was a panatella shape, long, thin,
and beautifully fresh to his fingers.

"I'll join you, with pleasure," she said, taking a
cigar, and he smiled at himself for not having offered
her the box.

He watched her smelling the barrel of the cigar,
then struck a lucifer and held the light for her.

"Delightful!" Her smile took over her whole face
as she leaned back, crossing her legs.

She was wearing a loose white silk tunic, and he
was sure she had nothing on underneath, for when
she'd leaned forward, he'd easily caught the projec-
tion of a prominent nipple. His blood raced. She was
wearing mocha-colored riding breeches, so tight that,
to his delight, every line showed. Around her waist
she wore a sash, Russian-style. And she wore riding
boots, highly polished, tooled, and expensive. She
was expensive all over, especially on her jeweled
fingers, wrists, and the lobes of her smallish ears.
Her hair was long, blue-black, and arranged on top
of her head in a style he had never seen. Once, when
she reached up both hands to tuck some random
wisps, her nipples quivered through the silk blouse
and she caught his stare.

She had raised her glass. "I do hope you like
Drambuie. It's really an after-dinner libation or, as
you say in this country, a drink. But it needs to be
taken slowly."

Slocum was seated in an armchair with a cowhide
seat, leaning forward with his elbows on his knees,
his glass in one hand, the cigar in his other. "I do
believe in drinking Drambuie slowly," he said. "In
fact, I like to do quite a few things slowly."

He was watching her eyes as he spoke. They were dark, almost black, and in the soft light of the room they seemed to sparkle now and again. "Do you have a first name?" he asked suddenly. "Or do I just call you Godiva?"

"You can call me Stefanie, since I hope to count you amongst my friends."

"I hope so too," Slocum said, and he felt his pulse quicken. There was something really animal about her. When she moved, she seemed to make no sound at all, yet at the same time he felt that her body must be purring. He had early noted the slight darkness in her skin and wondered if she had Indian blood or perhaps black.

He wondered, too, why Humboldt Smithers in his rundown of the interesting people in town had failed to mention Lady Godiva. But his thoughts were immediately pulled away from Humboldt as his hostess said, "I expect you're wondering why I wanted to see you." And then she threw back her head, and laughter rippled along her neck as her teeth flashed in the light of the coal-oil lamps. Slocum wondered why she didn't have gas lamps. Maybe she liked a room that was darker, softer. In any event, the Drambuie tasted damn good.

"Why are you laughing?" he asked, cocking his head to one side.

"Because I almost said 'sent for you' instead of 'wanted to see you,' and I can imagine how that would have been received!" And again she laughed.

Suddenly she stopped, put down her drink, laid her cigar in an ashtray, and folded her hands on her knees. "I want to offer you a job," she said. "Oh, no, please hear me out. I know you're busy. A man like you has to be. But listen. This will pay well." She looked down at the back of her hand and, with her eyes still down, spoke. "I might go as far as to say you could name your price." And her eyes, which now seemed to him violet, snapped up to meet his. He thought she looked like a tiger.

"I'm listening, but it won't do you any good."

He noticed that while he had hardly touched his drink, she had almost finished hers.

"I need a man around the house." Her eyes and one hand swept the room to indicate a large enterprise.

"A bouncer? Strong-arm? Gun-whipper?"

"That and more. A manager. A man with brains, good sense."

"Sorry."

"I'll meet any price you name."

He was shaking his head slowly.

"I see you can do things slowly, just as you said." There was a teasing smile dancing in her eyes. She stood up. "Let me show you what I can do slowly. You shake your head. Watch what I can shake."

She began a little movement of her torso, staying right where she was in front of the sofa, with her feet not moving, and as her movements became more loose, more fluid, her blouse opened, and suddenly her shoulders were bare. Now the white silk began to slip down as she undulated before his staring eyes. It was an extraordinary dance, no question about that for Slocum, and without music. But none was needed.

The blouse now slipped onto her breasts, which held it for moments, and then it worked to her waist. A pair of creamy, high, vigorous teats were springing right in front of his eyes and his bulging cock. All the while she kept her eyes right on him, smiling, teasing, tickling him with her sideways glances, her little laughter.

"I'll bet you can't get the rest off like that," he said, having just a little trouble speaking.

"I'll bet I can't, too," she said, her voice like satin, "so you'd better help me."

Slocum was only too glad to oblige.

Slocum could see that Horse Creek was not recovering easily from the tragedy: the double murder and rape, followed by the suspicious lynching of Dummy Jensen. A lot of people to whom he had talked seemed to feel that Dummy had been murdered, that justice had not been upheld, and that the men involved—and nobody appeared to be absolutely sure who they were—had acted hastily. Then, too, some were clearly afraid to speak up, to voice any accusation that might point to Dummy having been the innocent victim of mob violence.

Slocum could see that the anticipated herd of steer and their accompanying Texas cowboys was helping to soften the bitter pill for a good many, especially those in the way of business. And there would be more herds, and more of an influx of people coming into Horse Creek. But this, of course, would make it all the easier then for Cherokee Bill Hagstrom to slip in to town without a ripple and wreak his ghastly vengeance. On—who? Anyone he might suspect of having a hand in killing his brother. Nor would Cherokee allow doubt to question his hand. In a word, nobody was safe. Slocum saw this quite clearly, as did Colonel Humboldt Smithers. The town, as such, of course gave no voice to such fear, but all felt it. That fear was tangible. As the Colonel put it, you could reach out and touch it with your hand.

And it was again and again remembered that no one, at least among the living, had ever had a close look at Cherokee Bill. He pillaged at night, and his face was always covered with a bandanna.

As Slocum had himself discovered, the citizens of Horse Creek were suspicious of every stranger who rode into town. Since they were dependent on much of their business with passing strangers, this made things difficult.

An immigrant complained bitterly to the unsmiling bystanders in the Ajax Feed and Hardware Store who never took their eyes off him while he was making his purchases. Others voiced antagonism toward the suspicious glances, and even mutterings.

Buffalo skinners and trail hands who drifted into Horse Creek for a fling at the saloons and cribs were watched closely. This caused a number of bloody fights.

"It's getting to be ridiculous," Humboldt Smithers told Slocum one day. "They'll start shooting their shadows anytime now."

"And it's going to be that much worse with the Texans filling the town," Slocum pointed out. "Be easy as grease for Hagstrom to slip in unbeknownced."

"And out again after he's done what he's planning on doing," put in the Colonel.

"I'd be interested to know who the lynch party actually was," Slocum said.

"I got a pretty good idea," Humboldt said swiftly, "but I wouldn't want to back it in a court of law." He sniffed. "I take it you're figuring Cherokee will find out the names and go for them directly."

"I don't know. I'm not concerned with them; I want to locate Hagstrom."

"Gotcha." The Colonel beamed, stroked his long mustache carefully and with pleasure, and then spoke. "The town council would be a good bunch to keep an eye on. He'll surely look them up, even if he doesn't suspect them of doing the lynching. He'll likely get hold of one or two and torture the truth out of them, knowing from what I hear of him."

"And if they don't have the truth in them?" Slocum asked.

The Colonel shrugged, spread his hands open. "Then he'll just torture them."

"I believe I'll take a close look at those men," Slocum said. "And Kenton. The girl's father. I'd like to talk to him."

"I don't think he'll know anything," Humboldt said. "I don't believe he was a part of that mob."

"But he might have heard something from someone, a giveaway kind of thing."

The Colonel grinned. "Like he mightn't know that he knows something, or saw something, you're meaning?"

"Since people would be feeling for him in a certain way, something could have slipped out."

"It's worth a play."

"That is what I am telling you."

Slocum caught the foxy look on the Colonel's face. He waited.

"Don't overlook his girl," Humboldt said, making his face go serious again.

"Girl?"

"Norah's older sister, Kelly."

"There any others in the family."

"That's it. Annie, the mother, died a while back. Only Tom and Kelly now. She's a—a special person."

"You've got something on your mind."

"Only that I wouldn't want her hurt. You know, there's gossip all over the territory about what happened. I get it from news that comes in, and from news people dropping by. It's even causing some laughs how the town's scared of strangers—meaning Cherokee Bill could be anyone, right? And stories spread like that buffalo skinner who was braced in the Double Dice, somebody thinking he was Cherokee Bill, and he even had to show his papers to a bunch who gathered and would have shot him maybe if he hadn't been able to prove who he really was!"

Slocum nodded. "I heard about that."

"It's that kind of dumb thing. Somebody—Jeff Billings—making a horse's ass of himself and giving the town a dumb name, a laughingstock thing." He went on grumbling in his mustache.

Slocum had the feeling that the Cherokee Bill situation was rapidly getting out of hand. And when the cattlemen and cowboys got to town, it would be that much worse. Who knew who would be gunning down someone "suspicious"?

"Looks to me like you caught yourself an interesting job, Mr. Slocum—I mean, if I am hearing what you've been telling me between the lines." And the Colonel lowered both eyelids in a sly double wink.

4

The drummer was a great storyteller, like many who were members of his profession. Fletcher Schofield was even better than damn good, everyone in the Cheyenne Happy Saloon agreed. Right now he was telling about the scene that took place in the Double Dice back in Horse Creek where the buffalo skinner was braced by one of the townsfolk thinking he was Cherokee Bill Hagstrom. This brought a marvelous reaction from the listeners; the way Schofield told it, acting out the parts, even changing his voice, revealing the fear of the crowd in the bar and the stupidity of the man who had finally challenged the skinner.

"Damn lucky that skinner was drunk as a un-watched Puritan," Schofield was saying in conclusion. "Sober, he could've taken that asshole who braced him with just one cut." And he made a slicing motion with his hand, as though it were holding a skinning knife. The crowd in the saloon roared in appreciation.

Except for one man, sitting in the background at a table that supported only a half-empty bottle of trail whiskey and his two elbows. His brow was wrinkled; he was obviously deep in thought.

Meanwhile the drummer had finished his long and highly colorful story and the crowd had resumed their happy drinking. The loner at the table remained sunk in thought. So deep was his thought that he was even ignoring the whiskey that stood to hand. He was a big man and best described as filthy. No one thought this strange, however, since he was a wolfer. Shortly he was joined by two more who looked quite like him, though slightly smaller. All three smelled foul, were caked with dirt, grease, and filled with obvious contempt for anyone within range of their vision. They were probably enjoying the fruits of their recent operation in which they had put a great deal of time and effort living outdoors under frightful conditions of heat, cold, storm, and danger from Indians, wild animals, and each other while they got their wolves.

The wolfers followed after the buffalo hunters and skinners. The buffalo carcasses that were left on the prairie stank with the same intensity as did the three at the table. Only the carcass was left; the tongue, which was a prized delicacy in the restaurants of the West—and even back East—and, of course, the hide had been removed. The corpses lay rotting on the prairie while the wolfers seeded them and the area immediately surrounding with pellets of strychnine. The wolves who followed the buffalo herds would find the carcasses and would start to feast. It was inevitable that they would encounter the poison. Thus the wolf was followed by the wolfer, who took its pelt to market; predator following predator.

"Felix, what you thinking? You playing with

yourself again?" one of the three wolfers asked as Felix, his brow still wrinkled, scratched vigorously in his crotch.

"Fuck yourself," Felix said.

The wolfer who had spoken spat copiously, not even trying to hit the cuspidor, and almost spraying the third man, who clearly didn't mind at all.

"Fuck myself, eh?" Lolly, the one who had almost hit his companion—whose name was Bile—cleared his nose and throat loudly, hawked, and this time drove a fistful of phlegm, spit, tobacco juice, and who knows what else at the cuspidor, almost drowning that poor household article. "That's my best offer so far today," he went on philosophically. "Shit . . . I sure could use something right now."

"What you mean right now?" Bile said with a hard laugh. "You want it all the time, for chrissake!"

"Don't you?"

"Bet your ass and balls on that, boy!" Bile dropped a big wink, lowering a dirt-encrusted eyelid slowly over his right eye, then raising it slowly.

This brought a round of laughter from Lolly, but their companion, Felix, remained gray in thought.

"Shut up," Felix said suddenly, as he sensed their questioning. "Shut up! I am figuring on something."

"Figurin' some pussy!"

"Figurin' on how we can make ourselves a shitpot full of money, you stupid bastards!" Felix made this statement without any rancor whatever, as though he were simply stating the weather or the time. And the comment was received in a similar vein by his two comrades.

They sat silently in the saloon, which was quieter since the drummer had left.

Felix leaned forward, throwing a quick glance at a nearby table where a desultory poker game was in progress. But no one appeared to be noticing the three wolfers; probably they'd gotten used to the smell.

Even so, Felix spoke in a low tone, leaning close to his companions. "I got a notion here," he said. He nodded toward the bar where the drummer had been holding court. "Somethin' that feller said, the one with the pigeon ass."

"The drummer..." put in Lolly, and fell to sucking his teeth, which were large, protruding, and streaked with brown and yellow.

Felix grunted. "He was tellin' about the doin's at that shitty little town. You recollect?"

"Hoss Creek," Bile said. And his beard opened to reveal a few teeth—most were missing—in what was otherwise a dark, foul-smelling cavern. He was grinning. "Sure won't never forget that fun for this good while," he said.

"I got a idee how to have some more fun and make some money."

"Girls? Women?" Lolly leaned forward, bracing his great weight on his forearms, which lay across each other on the table in front of his chest.

"No girls!" snapped Felix darkly. "That is out. I am talking about big money. . . . You assholes want to hear it?"

"Sure as hell do," said Lolly. And Bile nodded several times, his breath whistling eagerly through his beard.

"Then go get another bottle and bring it over to that corner table." Felix stood up. He was well over six feet and broad in the shoulders. "C'mon. Move yer asses. 'Tend to business now!"

The hitch racks were crowded, so Slocum decided on the livery stable, but then he saw a place outside the Double Dice, which stood between the Ajax Feed and Hardware and the Wild Horse Eatery.

A heavyset man wearing yellow galluses and a wide leather belt greeted him as he walked into the big store.

"I am needing some ammo," Slocum said, approaching the worn wooden counter.

Parker Tilbury's eyes flicked to the holstered .45. "For the Colt?" His air was friendly, his thin hair was combed close to his head, and he had big hands with hardly any definition between the knuckles. This detail was noted by Slocum as the storekeeper pushed his wares forward on the counter.

"Two boxes will do for now," Slocum said. "And two for the Winchester," he added. ".44-.40."

"First time in this part of the country?" Tilbury asked pleasantly. He was an expansive man; his body was big, but his skin seemed even bigger, hanging on his large frame almost as though it had been draped over him. He breathed heavily.

He flushed a little as his customer accepted the ammunition and paid out money without answering his question.

"Quiet in town," he resumed, trying to pick it up again. "'Course, it'll be livelier than a man can imagine once the Texans get here."

"You figurin' on that soon?" Slocum asked.

"Anytime now. Three, four days, I'd reckon. My name's Parker Tilbury. I got an idea you're the one the boys in the Three Aces mistook for our famous outlaw."

"Can you tell me how the grub is in that beanery you got next door?" Slocum asked.

Parker Tilbury forced a smile to cover his irritation. "The best, I'd say. I recommend it. Eat there myself more than just often."

"They got a good cook, huh?"

"Like I said, the best. Kelly Kenton runs the place. I've known Kelly since she was knee-high to a pussycat." He nodded in agreement with himself. "Yep. Kelly is a first-class cook, first-class everything. I have known her dad Tom since before she was born."

Slocum started moving toward the door. "Good enough," he said. "I'll give the menu a whirl."

Parker Tilbury stood in the open doorway of his store. "I'm a councilman here in Horse Creek; and this here is my store." He let a little laugh drift out of his loose face. "Just want you to know you're welcome here. Name's Parker Tilbury."

Slocum nodded and stepped out onto the walk. He felt the storekeeper watching his back as he started toward the Wild Horse Eatery. He had known all along, since talking to Humboldt Smithers, that Kelly Kenton ran the eatery, and he didn't have any particular need for ammunition at that moment, but he had wanted to see some of the men Humboldt had told him about, some of the council, and without exciting comment. He also wanted to meet Kelly Kenton, Norah's older sister. He had a notion that he could help his search for Cherokee Bill by getting to know the principals in the drama of Dummy Jensen.

The Wild Horse Eatery was deserted when he

walked in. But something was cooking in the kitchen; he heard the sound of a pot or pan coming through the open door at the back of the counter. There were tables, and he hesitated, then decided on one in the corner. The counter wouldn't suit his purpose, for if he could engage Kelly Kenton in conversation, he would prefer some privacy.

He had just taken his hat off and sat down when the girl came in from the kitchen.

"The menu smells real good," he said, smiling at her as she approached his table. "How about a steak, not cooked too much; some eggs, fried; and spuds. Coffee."

"Yes, sir!"

Her crisp tone gave him a jolt; then he realized that she was imitating him.

"You got that right?" he said severely as she scribbled on her pad.

"Yes, sir! Fried spuds not cooked too much, a boiled egg, and a burned steak. And—a glass of milk."

And she was gone, leaving behind a whisk of perfume that delighted him, plus the vision of a profile of wavy brown hair, a tilted nose, a dimple, and the curve of a delicious breast. Her retreating rear was nothing to overlook, either, he noted, laughing quietly to himself as he settled into his chair.

When he saw her briefly through the open door to the kitchen, he called out, "Can I have the coffee now?"

Almost on the instant, she appeared with his coffee mug. "Consider it done, sir!"

"Hey. . ." he called as she started off without so much as a glance at him.

"Do you really want me to burn that steak? You'd better let me go." She had stopped and turned to face him.

She had large brown eyes that looked a trifle sad and, at the same time, slightly amused. A young lady with a heartache trying to cover it with humor. Slocum was touched.

He was also impressed by her looks, her figure, and the way she was reacting to him. Furthermore, he was discovering a great excitement in his trousers.

When she returned with his food, he said, "I reckon you're Kelly Kenton."

"I reckon that too."

"Got a minute to sit down?" he asked, with a quick glance toward the door to see that there were still no customers.

"Sure." She could have been twenty-four, twenty-five.

"My name's John Slocum."

"My spy system already informed me of that fact. What can I do for you, Mr. Slocum?"

"Just wanted to make your acquaintance. The man running the feed store told me you had good grub here. He didn't tell me how good-looking the cook was, however."

"You want to ask about my sister, don't you," she said simply.

He watched her mouth tighten as she spoke.

"No," he said. "Not really." He watched how she didn't react to that, at least not visibly, and then he said, "I'd like to invite you to supper this evening. Not here, though—maybe at the Denver House."

This brought her out of the emotion that had started up in her, which had been his purpose.

"I'm sorry," she said. "Another time." And she stood up.

"I'll ask you again," Slocum said.

She was standing looking directly at him now, and all at once he could feel himself falling right into her deep brown eyes. By God, he told himself, he hadn't felt that kind of experience in this good while. It was a shock to realize what he'd been missing.

He could see she was about to say something, but the door opened then and a man walked in asking for coffee as he sat down at the counter.

For a few moments Slocum watched her moving about, getting the coffee. She moved gracefully, keeping well inside herself, and he appreciated that. He finished his coffee and dessert of apple pie and stood up and walked to the front of the counter, away from the other customer.

When she came, he paid his bill and then said, "Miss Kenton, if you ever need anything—that I can do—please don't hesitate. I think I'll be around town for a while."

She was looking directly at him as she said, "Thank you, Mr. Slocum." And he could see the tears tingling behind her eyes. But she didn't let them out. "I will remember that."

"And I will be asking you for supper again."

She said nothing to that but waited there while he left, closing the door quietly behind him.

"We all realize, of course, that with all the Texans in town, as well as others who will be attracted once we're known for a cattle depot, that Cherokee Bill Hagstrom can slip in very, very easily."

Ed Deal watched their faces fall as his words dropped somberly across the round table.

He only let it numb them up to a point, then he said, "We need a tough man for marshal."

"An honest John Law," intoned Clem Dunstan with a sly grin.

But Deal took it straight, and there was no smile on his face as he said, "Not honest. Tough. Straight with us, but we don't care what he does otherwise."

"Are you going to tell us who you have in mind, Ed?"

Ed Deal leaned back, his eyes covering each one of the council in turn. "John Slocum," he said.

Tod Ollenburgh whistled between his teeth, staring down at his glass of whiskey. Parker Tilbury scratched his head. Dunstan scratched his crotch, and John Bettman looked at Deal, who met his eyes and then turned to the others.

"That'd be a tough one, Ed, I'd allow," Bettman said. "How we gonna handle him? That man's all balls from what I hear."

"Just the man for the job," Deal said smoothly. "Just the kind. Tough."

"I have heard he rode with Quantrill," Tilbury said.

"True. And he was sharpshooter with Pickett."

"He is no psalm singer, and that's a gut." Clem Dunstan dropped a fat chuckle onto the table as he leaned forward to pick up his glass of whiskey.

"But what if he finds out something we don't want him to find out?" Ollenburgh put in. "That could happen."

"The point is, we want him to find the real killer if there was one. The real rapist," Deal said.

"But . . ." Ollenburgh opened his hands in an offering gesture.

"But what?" Deal came back at him. "Suppose he
finds the real killer, since maybe it wasn't Dummy. I
say maybe. Or suppose he finds nothing. We're in
the clear no matter which way it goes. The point I'm
making is that we hire Slocum just for that purpose
—to find that Dummy Jensen was or was not the
killer and rapist. If not, then somebody—I say,
somebody—made a 'mistake.' And if he comes up
with the real killer, we'll be heroes. We'll help Slocum all the way. Remember, we're paying his sal-
ary."

"Jesus," whispered somebody. No one was certain
who, for they were all tight in their thoughts.

A long silence covered the room as the four men
contemplated what Deal had said to them. Bettman
started at one point to speak but stopped.

Ed Deal took it up. "We need Slocum. Can you
see that? We need Slocum to stand between us and
Hagstrom. He is our—well, you might say, our extra
protection."

"That's a great idea, Ed," agreed Parker Tilbury,
"but how will you keep him in line? He's an indepen-
dent son of a bitch, I have been told. And I have seen
it too."

A thin smile reached Ed Deal's pale face as he
listened to Tilbury. It was the final objection and easily disposed of. "That's easy," he said, the thin line
of his lips extending further as he prepared his convincer. "That's a simple matter. I happen to know
that Slocum is a wanted man in Big Horn County."

He smiled fully now as he saw their eyes open to
this news.

"You're saying the law is after him," Ollenburgh said.

"Right. Something he was involved in during the cattle troubles up in Big Horn. Messy. There are flyers on him but not around this part of the country. And—and I have my contacts who keep me up on the news. No, gentlemen, rest assured, I wouldn't hire John Slocum or anyone, actually, that I couldn't handle."

And now Ed Deal's smile was suddenly contagious. The others relaxed visibly. Somebody poured more liquor. Cigars were relighted, and Parker Tilbury shifted his Stetson hat farther back on his head.

Then John Bettman thought of something. "But has Slocum agreed? Will he go along?"

"I haven't spoken to him yet," Deal said, with a more private smile now as he looked down at a spot on his vest where some whiskey had dripped from his glass. "But I am sure he will. After all, it's us or the marshal of big Horn and the Cattle Growers Association. That's not really a difficult choice for a sensible man. Wouldn't you say so?"

The Colonel was in form; that is to say, he was expansive, and even more loquacious than usual. Slocum had hardly drawn up a chair in the Double Dice before Humboldt was off on another story, this one about Lady Godiva, before she was known as Lady Godiva, when she was a barmaid named Myrtle back in Red Rock in the Platte country and one day some miners braced her.

"Seems these fellers, they was about four of them, was pretty well liquored and were standing at the bar betting on anything—I mean, anything. Like, for instance, how many swallows someone at a certain table would take to finish his drink. Things like that. Godiva got into it, and the long and short was she, by Jehosophat, bet she could strip and walk the length of the room and back and not a man in the place would make a sound. Now what d'you think of that?"

"Were you there?" Slocum asked.

"I was there! Godiva, in those days, was a damn good-looking kid."

"In those days? She's pretty damn good-looking now," Slocum said.

"Heh-heh! I hear authority in your tone of voice, young man." And a rumbling laugh came all the way up through the Colonel's cavernous throat and out into the room. It was so loud, heads turned.

"Just passing through," Slocum said, his face the picture of innocence.

"I'll bet that girl can screw a man right through the floor and still be ready for more," the Colonel said.

"I wouldn't know."

"You mean you're not telling. But no matter. No matter!" Humboldt lifted a protesting hand and swept on with his story.

"Well, they took the bet. There was a old geezer there who covered it and raised it. And, of course, there was the four miners. Godiva was just the bar- maid, but there was a big bouncer feller there in the bar, also serving drinks, and he held the purse."

"Come on," said Slocum, laughing. "Get to the point. What happened?"

"Simple. She did it."

"She walked naked the length of the room and back, and not a man said anything."

"That is what I am saying."

"No whistle, even?"

"Not a one."

"Did anyone grab her?"

"They sure as hell didn't."

"Well, then, she was carrying something."

The Colonel wagged his head, snapping his fingers. "Dadburn it, Slocum. I might have known you'd figure it."

He looked so crestfallen, like a little child, that Slocum burst out laughing.

"Where was this—at Red Rock? That's a tough country."

"Godiva ducked behind the bar. Stripped to nothing! Jesus, what a body! When she stepped out from back of that bar, I thought we were all going to pass out or jump her—one. Excepting she was carrying a shiny, new, and not at all pretty-looking Colt .45."

"Figures," Slocum said, grinning. "She's a lady who knows how to cover her bets."

"She is no lady to get previous with," Humboldt said. "I am just warning you. But I can tell you have already met same. And good luck to you."

The Colonel did look somewhat dashed from Slocum having anticipated the punch line of his story. "'Course, there are more stories about her than you can shake a stick at," he said, rallying. "Let me—"

"Later," Slocum said. "I mean, save them. One good story at a time is enough. You know, it takes time to swallow it all."

"Just wanted to let you know about the man-eater who came to town here a few years back."

"Tell me about Kelly Kenton," Slocum said.

The Colonel's blue eyes danced with merriment, his good humor wholly restored. "Ah, you lascivious creature of the mountains and plains. Slocum, not my business, mind you, but I daresay you have had more than your share of women out here in God's country, and you're still a young man! But, no matter, no matter. . . ." And once again the protesting hand was raised to stem any possible objection, attack, or argument from his companion, who had no intention of saying anything at all on the particular subject.

"How long have you known Tom Kenton?" Slocum asked.

But the Colonel never had a chance to answer him, for the swinging doors of the saloon burst open and old Karl, the saloon's swamper, burst in. He was highly agitated to the point where he was having trouble breathing.

His words cracked into the suddenly frozen room. "Jock Kramer and Bill Wellman was found dead out on the trail to Holton. The stage brought 'em in. Cal Whipple spotted them lying on the trail not far from their soddy. He was riding shotgun, thought they was a decoy for the road agents. But they was dead— dead—dead!"

The tale of horror broke from old Karl as though it were his last testament. Indeed, having finished, he broke down and wept. And Slocum heard the name of Cherokee Bill Hagstrom passing through the room.

"My God," said Humboldt, rising slowly to his

feet, as though the awesome event had actually drawn him up out of his chair.

Slocum said nothing. He was searching his memory for those names, for they held a familiar ring.

"I think I must get to my office," the Colonel said. "I have to think this thing out."

"Those names are familiar."

"They are, indeed. You will remember that I mentioned to you that there were two men who defended Dummy Jensen with their statements as to his whereabouts at the time of the tragedy."

"One was rubbing down a horse."

"Jock Kramer that was, the livery hostler. Dummy was helping him. And Bill Wellman spoke up for Dummy, saying he'd beaten the wrangler who insulted Norah, but that didn't prove he'd killed and raped her."

"And they both are dead."

"They were friends—Bill and Jock. Batched together ever since they'd done some panning on Crazy Woman Creek. I guess maybe Cherokee might have gotten his signals crossed. Maybe he thought they was in on the lynching of his brother."

"Or maybe somebody else doesn't want them to talk," Slocum said.

Slocum knew it was no accident when the man with the sleek black hair and sleek black clothing—frock coat, tight trousers—evinced surprise at running into him in the Denver House dining room.

"You must be John Slocum, sir!"

"Is that a question or a statement of fact?" Slocum had asked quietly as the man paused at his table.

"I'm Ed Deal. I'm on the town council, and I also function as mayor and the town banker."

Slocum knew who Deal was, had known him by sight, the Colonel having pointed out all the council members to him at some time or another.

"I see you're at the end of your meal, sir. Might I sit for a moment?"

Slocum nodded toward the vacant chair opposite him. Deal was neat in his movements, and Slocum put him down as a careful, tidy man who knew how to plan and stick to details. He also noted the pallor of the man's complexion and the coldness around his mouth and eyes.

Deal looked around for a place to put his derby, then, finding none, started to place it in his lap. But Slocum reached over to the next table and brought round one of the chairs.

"Thank you, sir." The banker sighed, and Slocum took note of the fact that Deal had not mentioned that he was also the sole undertaker in town.

"What can I do for you, then?" Slocum said, reaching to his shirt pocket for a quirly.

"I did want to talk with you, Slocum. . . ." Deal pursed his lips softly, and then raised his eyebrows as though trying to adjust his sight. "Uh—your presence in town has been—well, noticed, let me put it that way. In an agreeable way," he added swiftly. "And, of course, you have been brought to my attention by my associates on the council."

"You could get to the point," Slocum said, striking a wooden match on his thumbnail.

"Sure. Of course." The words came quickly as Deal tried to cover his annoyance at Slocum taking the lead. But he recovered quickly and said, "I want to put some facts before you, Slocum. But"—he looked around the room—"I think it would be much better if you could come to my office. I don't wish to be overheard."

"I don't think anyone can overhear you here," Slocum said. "Why don't you just tell me what you want?" He waited a beat and then stood up. "Let's go to the saloon. This place is stuffy."

Deal was on his feet, a laugh—a genuine laugh —coming out of him. "That's a good compromise, Slocum. And, mind you, I like a man of action!"

They reached the Three Aces in a matter of minutes, with no further conversation along the way.

Oren the bartender brought a bottle to a back room, and Slocum was glad to see that the brand was different from the usual. Nice to have powerful acquaintances, he reflected, at least now and again. And he thought of Humboldt Smithers and what sort of tight comment he would make if he knew of the present meeting. Slocum was beginning to get an idea of what Deal might have in mind.

"So you want me to work for you, is that it?" And he came right out with it before Deal had hardly settled into his chair and reached for the bottle.

Ed Deal sat back in his chair with surprise on his face. "I heard you were a shrewd one, Slocum."

Slocum was thinking of Godiva and her offer, wondering if she and Deal were connected.

"I just turned down a pretty fair offer of a job," he said now. "So I don't mind turning down yours."

"Why not wait till you hear what I have to say." Deal's voice was just slightly tinged with irritation. But he smiled in an attempt to cover it. "You were right about my wanting to offer you a job, but you don't know, you cannot know, what that job is. Besides, it isn't just for me that you'd be working."

Slocum lifted his glass and studied the reflection of the room's light in the amber fluid. "I am listening."

"I—the town council—want you to be marshal of Horse Creek."

No, he sure hadn't expected that, but he showed no surprise on his face, nor in his general manner.

Deal didn't wait for him to respond but went on. "This town, as you must know, is expecting a big Texas herd. Its first. And there are others coming. There is no law here, and we're going to need it. We need a strong man, and an honest one. We believe you fill the holster on that, Slocum."

"I've been a lawman," Slocum said. "It isn't my kind of life."

But Deal was riding his point and swept on. "Then there's this unfortunate business over the Jensen boy. Dummy, he was called, because the poor lad was deaf and dumb. You've undoubtedly heard about it."

"I've heard not much else in a certain way," Slocum said.

Deal stared at him. "How do you mean that? I don't understand."

"It's not what anyone has said especially, but you can tell it's on most people's minds. I'm talking about Cherokee Bill Hagstrom."

"Yes, there is indeed some concern here, since he is known as a very successful, not to say vicious, road agent, cattle rustler, bank robber, a murderer, and who knows what else." Deal wagged his head slowly. "All the more reason for us to have a town marshal who isn't afraid of such types and who will act in the name of justice!" He sat back, drumming his fingers lightly on the table.

"You're going to need more than a town marshal," Slocum said. "What with the Texans whoop-de-doin' and maybe figuring to tree the town, and you've also got those fellers who lynched Dummy Jensen. What about them—eh?"

"Those men too," Deal said easily, carefully keeping his eyes on Slocum. "If they did wrong, then they must be brought to justice. If not, then they have nothing to worry about."

Slocum said nothing. He slowly took a drink, then leaned forward with his elbows on the table and looked right at Ed Deal. He had to admit to himself that the idea appealed to him in a certain way. It could help him in his search for Cherokee Bill, for one thing. And it could also help him to clear up the murder of Norah Kenton and her boyfriend, and so take care of something for Kelly Kenton. He didn't mind helping a decent person like Kelly; and he knew it wasn't only because she excited him sexually. The poor girl had to be going through hell. He wanted to help her. And maybe he could. He hadn't thought of this kind of job offer but rather something along the lines of what Godiva had offered him. Yes, it might be interesting and help him all round. He was suddenly certain that Deal and Godiva were working together; that she'd been sounding him out with her offer.

"I want to make something clear," he said now as Deal started to speak.

There was a smile on the banker's face. "You want a free hand."

"That is correct."

"I would agree that would be the only way you could work the job," Deal said amiably. He lifted his glass of whiskey. "It's settled, then?"

Slocum lifted his glass. "It's a deal," he said. And he noted the droll relationship of the word he'd used with the banker's name. For at that same moment he had a feeling that Deal had agreed too easily to his demand for a free rein. Yes. Deal had something up his sleeve—another card. Well, he would go along and he would see. The banker's bland impartiality in regard to his "freedom" in the proposed marshal's job and also in regard to Dummy Jensen's lynchers fooled him not at all. And for an instant the thought crossed his mind that Deal might know about Big Horn. In his position, the man must have contacts— he was that kind.

5

It was evening, the sun was down, but there was still that lingering light in the foothills and on the plain. And the air had cooled as it always did at that altitude. In the town, lights had gone on here and there. The office of the *Horse Creek Gazette* was busily active as Colonel Humboldt Smithers and his helper, a lad named Tracy Timms, got out the latest edition of the paper. The saloons were doing their usual business, and in many of the homes people were getting ready for supper. But everyone was aware that in only a day or two the great Texas herd was due. In fact, a rider had already reached town in advance of the cattle and cowboys with news that the J. C. Klanghorn herd had just crossed the south fork of the Stingwater. A day, two at most, would get them to the new shipping point.

The three riders rode quietly toward the town. It was nearly dark now, and as they approached the edge of Horse Creek, coming in through that area known as the Cabbage Patch, they still seemed to be part of the darkness from which they had detached themselves. They rode, not close together but near enough for muted conversation. They could have been taken for point riders on the J. C. herd, or more possibly scouts. They rode on good horseflesh, their eyes flicking to the lighted windows of the cribs that lined the street through the Cabbage Patch.

"See anything?"

"Naw."

"How about stoppin'? I'm ready for a little greasing."

"No!" The word snapped out of the man riding on the right of his two companions. "I told you dumb shits already we wuz here on business only! Bile, you peel off up there ahead to the left, and Lolly, you ride in front of me. We don't wanta be so bunched together comin' in now."

Neither of them said anything to that but simply did as bidden. Felix was nobody to argue with, they each knew; Lolly carrying a scar near his groin as evidence of same, and Bile minus his left earlobe. These wounds on Felix's two mates had been delivered while they were both attacking him at the same time. Felix was not only a master with his skinning knife, but he also handled a handgun like it was a part of him, another limb, a special hand. And fast. Bile said it took two to watch Felix in action—one to watch him start, the other to see him getting there.

"There it is," Felix said, just loud enough for his companions to hear.

The Last Drop Saloon and Dance Hall. As they drew toward it, the door burst open and the strident strains of fiddle and cornet music hit the street in a rendition of "Chicken in the Breadtray." Laughter, curses, and the sound of jolly times broke the silence that had been the town's accompaniment to their ride in from the north.

They dismounted at the hitch rail, looking at the other horseflesh there, to see if anything was worth taking when they made their departure.

"All crow-bait stuff," Bile said in disgust as they walked toward the swinging doors.

"No." Felix stopped several feet away from the sound of the dance within. "You two come in later. Maybe five minutes apart, like by time I'm settled at the bar. Come in one at a time but stay near the door, not together! And cover me. Cover me good, but don't let on you're with me."

They waited while Felix walked through the swinging doors and into the Last Drop. When maybe five minutes had elapsed, Bile nodded his head toward his companion, and Lolly walked into the saloon.

Five minutes later Bile followed suit.

There was a large and lively group around the dice table in the Last Drop, pressing in on the players, and the big man who was running the game had to keep ordering the people back, to give the players room.

Slocum had been there a while, watching the big man. No doubt about it, he was gifted. He had little eyes and they were quick as mice, missing nothing. His most obvious trait to Slocum was his reflexes. He was loose as a snake; and Slocum, who always admired professionalism, took pleasure in studying him.

His name was Burgess, and Slocum watched him throwing in tops, palming the flats, then switching

back again as the play required. He was pretty sure
nobody else was wise to Burgess's manner of play.
At least not anyone with enough sand in his craw to
say so.

When the wolfer who had been drinking at the bar
stepped over to watch the game, Slocum knew trouble was coming. He'd seen the man walk in. Smelled
him. No question how he made his living. The
wolfers stank! And they were as dangerous, as vicious, as unpredictable as the animals they hunted.
Men moved slightly away from this one as he pushed
in toward the edge of the dice game.

The wolfer had clearly been drinking, yet that
wasn't to say he couldn't handle his liquor. But Slocum figured there was more than the man's wish to
just get into the game when he pushed in, for he'd
spotted the two other wolfers coming in separately
and staying close to the door. One was seated with
his drink at a table watching a game of three-card
monte; the other was seated alone with his chair
tipped back against the wall, very close to the bat-
wing doors. He was also holding a drink but not in
his gun hand.

Slocum had not yet taken on the formal office as
town marshal, he wasn't wearing any tin, and he
wasn't going to confront the three wolfers regarding
their armaments. There were other men in the room
wearing guns, even though there was the town law
that said all weaponry had to be checked either with
the marshal's office or with the bar one was fre-
quenting at the particular moment. During the time
without an active marshal in Horse Creek, things had
gotten lax.

Felix was standing right up against the dice table

now, right across from Burgess. It was obvious he was planning on joining the game. Slocum watched Burgess throw a glance at the wolfer. A cold glance, suspicious, likely wondering whether the newcomer had spotted his latest switch.

Slocum wondered, too, for Burgess was slick. Slocum had studied with a professional years ago, back in Denver; and he'd even gotten quite good— for an amateur—switching, palming the dice, now flats, now the tops with the spots so placed on them that no seven combination could ever be thrown. He waited now, watching the two men—the wolfer and the dice man, each well aware of the other. But the wolfer was in no hurry to get into the game. Slocum knew he was studying the dice man closely. And it was clear that Burgess knew it too.

Slocum lit a quirly and smiled to himself, letting his eyes roam over the room. The room seemed louder now as he drew his attention away from the table momentarily and looked about. It was important to be well aware of the surrounding setup when trouble was cooking; and Slocum was no novice to this situation. He looked again at the two wolfers by the door.

The room was really alive now with the wild jangle of the piano, the violins and banjo, and now and again the cornet, accompanied by the scraping sound of heavy boots; while intermittently, above the vibrancy of the instruments rose the "do-si-do" of the caller. Slocum was reminded for a brief moment of the fabled Alison Parker's palatial establishment in Denver, the last house of pleasure he had visited in a big city. Alison undoubtedly hostessed the supreme whorehouse of the Wild West, with truly good-look-

ing girls and with furnishings that evoked envy in
even the richest visitors; the thick red Brussels car-
pets, the fantastic chandeliers, the exquisite cut-glass
mirrors, the huge, ornate mahogany staircase down
which the delicious girls seemed to flow, and up
which their panting customers all but ran. No, the
Last Drop was a far holler and whimper from Alison's spectacular haven of bliss. Yet—and yet the
Last Drop had its attractions for Slocum. He was
always adaptable, always eager for whatever life had
to offer, especially when the deal was fun. There was
something about the Last Drop that he found to his
taste. Maybe it was the underlying pressure of excitement, violence, and the free flinging of some free
souls. It didn't matter. Even now, or maybe for all he
knew, especially now—with trouble brewing—he
felt more at home, less "safe," but also more alive.

When his attention returned to the game, he
watched the wolfer take a place at the table, and
when he got the dice, Burgess the houseman covered a couple of his throws with large bets, losing
one and winning the other.

When the wolfer passed the dice, Burgess came
out with a nine. He immediately offered to borrow
on the six-ace draw for five hundred.

"On nines and fives I always bet on the make,"
the wolfer said. His gravelly voice wasn't very loud,
but everybody heard it.

"I'll make it for five hundred."

"Make it for a thousand," Felix the wolfer said,
and he pulled out a handful of bills, peeled off a
number, and shoved them into the pot. The crowd
stirred.

A grin sliced across Burgess's face as he called, then rolled the dice.

Slocum edged closer. He knew this was going to be it.

The wolfer reached out and picked up the dice, and as he threw them back to Burgess, he said, "Two thousand you don't make it."

Burgess counted out the money while the crowd around the table fell silent in front of the drama that was unfolding.

Burgess threw, bumping the dice hard against the table railing. Before settling, they spun. It was the six-ace, and Burgess's face turned dark red under his muscular jowls.

Slocum saw that his right hand had moved toward the edge of the table. "You switched them dice, mister!"

Felix's voice was no less hard. "What you're sayin' is your dice were tops and couldn't make a six-ace!"

"You son of a bitch!"

But Felix had cut his eyes beyond the furious Burgess. While the crowd had moved back quickly to give the action plenty of room, Slocum saw that the two wolfers had moved in toward the table with their hands near their guns.

"Now, you wouldn't want to go up against the three of us, would you, mister?" And Felix nodded to Bile and Lolly. "I mean, not three pals of Cherokee Bill, now would you?"

The entire room had stopped, and the last words spoken by Felix fell like ice into the crowd's midst. Slocum saw Burgess turn white as his hand dropped down onto the table and moved no farther.

Somebody in the crowd hawked, clearing his nose, but thought better of it and didn't spit.

The wolfer, keeping his eyes right on Burgess, reached forward and picked up his winnings. Still watching the dice man, he pocketed the money.

Slocum had moved so that he had a clearer view of Felix's face, albeit in profile. The man was grinning. He was obviously rubbing it in. And looking at Burgess, Slocum wasn't sure how much the man could take, even with gunmen behind, even with the name Cherokee Bill still hanging in the loaded air.

Then, as the wolfer straightened up, right after pocketing his money, he reached again into his pocket, pulled out a silver dollar, and tossed it onto the dice table in front of Burgess.

"Something for your trouble," he said.

Slocum had been watching Burgess's eyes, and when he saw them tighten, he had the Colt in his hand.

"Right now!"

Burgess had dropped his hands onto the table in preparation for throwing himself at the wolfer. The two wolfers behind him froze in mid-action, their hands already on their gun butts. But the tone of Slocum's two words were not to be argued. Nobody even looked at the brindle cat who came from behind the bar and suddenly, silently, jumped up onto the dice table.

It was Burgess who found his voice. "Who the hell are you, stranger!"

"I'm the new marshal, mister. And there is a law in this town about no guns. You leave 'em in my office or at the bar—one. And you will start with that right now."

There was a stunned silence at this command, but once again nobody disputed it. There were only a very few in the crowd wearing guns, and these moved toward the bar, laying their weapons carefully on the scarred mahogany.

"Burgess and you three likewise," Slocum snapped. "I am saying right now!"

They were moving slowly toward the bar, the crowd giving plenty of room. Felix was the last to put his gun on the bar, and as he turned to follow his two companions out of the Last Drop, his eyes bore into Slocum.

"I don't see no tin star on you, mister."

"It's in my hand," Slocum said with a cold grin, and moved the barrel of the Colt just slightly in the direction of the swinging doors.

"When can we get our guns back?" Felix said.

"When you're ready to leave town." And as he saw Felix start back to the bar to get his gun, he added, "That will be in a while. You boys can just walk about some and cool off. Then come on down to my office and I'll give you your guns."

"Cherokee ain't gonna like the way you treat his friends."

"Then he can tell me personally," Slocum said. He watched them leave, the room still quivering with the name of Cherokee Bill Hagstrom in everyone's ears, not to mention guts.

Slocum turned then to Burgess. "You start running a straight dice game, Burgess—or I'll bust you sure as you're standing right here figuring on a 'next time.'" He grinned suddenly. "Just remember that this here is 'next time.'"

* * *

"That son of a bitch!"

The words came in bitter fury from Bile as the three wolfers huddled at their slim fire some miles out of town.

"The bastard needs some straightening out," added Lolly, reaching to his shirt pocket for the makings. "I mean, who the fuck he thinks he is—huh!"

Suddenly they realized that their companion was shaking. Silent laughter had taken over almost the whole of Felix's big body.

"What the hell's the matter with you!" Bile demanded. "It sure ain't somethin' to laugh. That man was not funnin' at all!"

With difficulty Felix's laughter subsided. "It sure is funny, you dumb shit heads! They fell for it. You could tell. The whole entire saloon fell for it. Even that stupid son of a bitch who I was tempted to, by God, take his peashooter and shove it up his ass! They all fell for it, all the way to the weddin'!"

His companions gasped. "Fell for what? What you talkin' about, Felix? You lost your head, have you?"

"They fell for it! And you dumb clowns, you knotheads don't even know what I am sayin'!"

"Fell for what? We all nearly got shot to hell by that goddamn marshal, that's what happened."

"Didn't you assholes hear what I said about Cherokee Bill?"

This stopped them head-on. They gaped at him with the firelight licking their filthy faces.

"Wondered why you said such a thing," Lolly said.

"Didn't know you had anything to do with that Cherokee man," Bile added.

"I never saw the gent in my life," said Felix, and his eyes disappeared in merriment as he shook again with silent laughter. "You buggers don't get it yet, for chrissake!"

"Get what? That you was making like you knew Cherokee?"

"That we did," put in Lolly.

"You got that, but neither one of you got the brains God promised a gopher." Felix leaned forward, rubbing a knuckle into one eye, still damp with his attack of the chuckles at his companions' amazement. "You don't get what's really going on. We're in the money now. We're rich."

"I still don't get it," said Lolly, lapsing into a sighing frustration.

"I see I got to spell it for you. You know, you are the both of you, by God, lucky as all hell to have somebody like me to do your thinkin' for you."

"You figured some way to bugger them townspeople, have you, Felix?" Bile's eyes were wide with the thought of money.

"Tomorrer I can go in there and mosey around and find out who was in on that lynching we heard about from that drummer feller in Cheyenne. See? He dropped a couple of names. We'll start there. I will. They'll be scared shitless and will be only too glad to hand over whatever I want."

"You mean . . . ?" Lolly was beginning to reach for it.

"Like you was . . ." added Bile, his breath catching with excitement.

"Cherokee Bill!" roared Felix, and his two companions roared it with him.

They spent most of the remaining night going

over the plan, talking, tasting it, feeling it all over, and then falling asleep and happily dreaming it.

It was late the following night when Clem Dunstan heard the knocking on his front door. He hadn't been asleep but had spent the two hours since going to bed lying beside Meg, his wife, his thoughts on the scene that he'd heard about in the Last Drop. He felt the blood pounding in his temples as he rose and went downstairs to the door.

"Who is it? What do you want?" he called through the door.

"You don't know me, mister. And I mean you no harm. I just want to tell you Cherokee Bill is your friend, but I want to find out who murdered my brother. Someone told me you could help me."

"I don't know. I sure didn't have anything to do with it." Clem Dunstan had trouble keeping his voice from shaking.

"But maybe you know who did?"

"I don't. I cannot help you. Please go away!"

"I'm a little short on money right now, Mr. Dunstan. Maybe you could help me out; and I won't bother you again. 'Fact, I'll forget all about what happened."

Some hours later Felix and his companions were roaring with laughter at their camp. The plan had worked like magic. They had visited three members of the town council. All had coughed up money.

"They was all scared shitless," Felix said, going over it again by the camp fire. Bile and Lolly had waited nearby just in case anything went wrong. But nothing had.

"Paid up like a baby asking for his milk," Lolly said, reciting it like a drone.

"Scared shitless, by God," Bile repeated, his voice soaked in awe at the marvelous good fortune that had befallen them.

"Where'll we be heading for now?" Lolly asked the next morning. "We got to do some spending. Have some fun with some things, some women."

They all agreed with that—the fun part. But Felix said they wouldn't be leaving the country.

"Why not?" Lolly asked, amazed at even the thought of remaining in a place where there was the risk of capture, or worse, a necktie party by their irate victims.

"We're going to lay low," Felix told them. "Wait and see if Cherokee shows up, then we can hightail it. Meanwhile we got our pigeons scared half to death. They won't tell on us, and if anyone does, it won't do 'em any good on account of they can't prove it. On account of this"—and he touched the bandanna hanging around his neck—"nobody saw me, they can only suspicion. Which is what we want. Scare 'em. They never saw my face. They think it was Cherokee Bill."

"So we'll hang around?"

"We'll hang around."

"But why?" Bile asked. "What in hell for? There is that marshal fucker. We don't want him messin' with us."

"I'll take care of him," Felix said. "Look, there is more where that came from." He patted his pocket. "A whole big lot more. And we ain't going to be bloody damn fools and pass it up. We'll wait a spell, let 'em think we're gone, see, left the country. Then we'll hit 'em again—but big this time. Big. Besides, we only hit three this time. There was more'n three in on that lynching!"

"But what about Cherokee?" said Bile. "What if he shows up?"

"Then he shows up. We didn't do nothin' to him. We'll keep a sharp eye out for him. If we get wind of him, then we can haul ass easy. Thing is, we'll keep out of sight for a spell. Move camp and don't get fixed. Let 'em worry on it. Then we'll slip in fast, get the best of it, and be long gone!"

The chuckle started deep in his chest and rumbled up into his throat, his eyes started to tear, and suddenly he was roaring with laughter, while Bile and Lolly joined in. It was impossible to refuse his merry mood. It was too much, too good. Not only the money, no, not just that. As they each kept pointing out between roars of laughter, it was more than the money. It was also the way they were pulling the wool over the eyes of this dumb town.

"But where did he get our names?" John Bettman brought his fist down hard onto the table. His long face was flushed, his eyes were wide with anger and maybe fear, Ed Deal thought as he watched him.

"Thing is," said Parker Tilbury, "was he really Cherokee Bill, or was he that feller we heard about in the Last Drop claiming he knew Hagstrom? Hell, I don't know what to think about it!"

"Well, I know what I think about it," Tod Ollenburgh cut in, clenching and unclenching his fingers nervously on top of the·table in front of him. "I don't want any more of this. We have got to do something.

I'm for laying the whole business out with Slocum. Hell, he is the marshal."

"But how far is he the marshal, the law?" Clem Dunstan said carefully. "Suppose we sic him on to this fellow—Cherokee or whoever he is, maybe that fellow he braced in the Last Drop said he was Hagstrom's friend—then he starts getting too close to the bone, if you catch what I am meaning."

"We don't want any lawman snooping around," Bettman said. "But we have got to do something. Who says he won't be back, wanting more! What the hell, next time he could call on you, Ed, and Parker. You were both lucky!"

Thus far only Ed Deal had not spoken. The mayor of Horse Creek sat quietly in his chair, seemingly unruffled, his hair combed down close to his head as it always was, his long, tailored hands and fingers touching the baize tabletop lightly, his head slightly bowed, giving the picture of close attentiveness to the speakers. But now all heads turned to him, his silence apparently having drawn them from their uneasy, angry rhetoric.

"What do you think, Ed?" It was Parker Tilbury who put the question, looking toward Deal, then down at his shirt cuff where he saw a long blond hair. Quickly removing it, he smiled inwardly as the image of the owner of that hair filled him. Well, there had to be more where that came from, that was for sure. And for a happy moment he had dropped the nagging problem of Cherokee Bill. But only for a very brief moment.

"There's no need to panic," Deal was saying. "We have done nothing to be ashamed of; let me repeat that, as I seem to have to do with you fellows every so often. We acted within the law. It could be we caught the wrong man. I say it could be. But I don't think so. But even if we'd made a mistake, is that a crime? Good heavens, no!"

"Agreed, Ed. I'm sure we all agree with that," Bettman said.

"Then why did you pay up?"

"But who would have known whether he might have killed any of us on the spot?" Tod Ollenburgh said, cutting in sharply.

"Or maybe had his gang with him. Ed, there were women and children involved. Our families." Clem Dunstan was leaning forward into the table, his fingers laced together hard.

"Right." Deal nodded in approval. "Just wanted to be clear, if anyone should ever question one of you, that you had a reason for paying up—and it wasn't because you felt guilty."

The suggestion of a sigh seemed to pass around the table. Ed Deal had a way of making things clear and simple. It was as though a load had been lifted. Momentarily. For there was still the possibility of a return of Cherokee Bill.

"We'll have to be very careful. Lock your doors. Keep a weapon handy, but make sure—very sure—before you pull the trigger."

At Crazy Woman Creek the J. C. herd was restive. They had reached this small strip of water the day before, and J. C. Klanghorn had ordered a halt. This caused a sweeping irritation to his cowboys who, following their tedious and difficult drive, and also in the time-honored tradition of all trail herders, were a

lot more than just eager to roar into town and wash
themselves clean in the attractions of Horse Creek.

But J. C. Klanghorn was not a man to be argued
with; he had other reasons for holding the herd than
just to allow them rest and a little fattening on that
good northern feed before driving them to Horse
Creek's new loading pens.

He stood now in the early-morning light under a
lowering sky listening to the bawling of the herd, a
tin cup of coffee in one hand and a chunk of sourdough bread in the other.

"Fixin' to storm some," Hendry Chimes, his trail
boss, observed, clomping up on his high-heeled
boots to stand there, letting his words come to J. C.
across a saddle rig that was lying on the ground close
by the chuck wagon.

"Mebbe." J. C. Klanghorn had squinted at the
low sky more than once. And he had his notion, but
he was a man of damn few words; true to the way of
that country, that time. A tall man, hardened by the
trail, the cattle herds, the Indian fighting, handling
the tough, the wild, and the vicious along the way.
His face was leather, and so were his hands. Someone had said that the leather went all the way through
him to the bone. His right eye was milky and the
thumb of his left hand was busted; both the result of
a barroom brawl with two buffalo skinners who tried
to take his woman of the evening. J. C.—and even
as a small boy he had been known as J. C.—had lost
the sight of his eye and the use of his thumb. The
buff skinners had lost their lives.

"Riders comin' in," Hendry Chimes said.

"I heerd 'em."

"Sounds like a pair, maybe three."

"It is three," J. C. said, and he rubbed the side of his hard jaw with his busted thumb. He was still holding the sourdough. "It'll be company."

He had just emptied his cup and dumped the grounds onto a clump of sage when the three riders rounded a stand of cottonwood and drew rein.

"You men et yet?" J. C. canted his head to one side in order to get full value from his good eye.

"Could stand a cup of coffee," Ed Deal said, coming down stiffly from his bay horse, while J. C. Klanghorn watched him critically and his trail boss, Hendry Chimes, sniffed.

His companions, Parker Tilbury and Clem Dunstan, followed suit. They were even more stiffened than Deal, and moreover, Tilbury had extra weight to contend with. At a sign from Deal, Tilbury and Dunstan moved off with Hendry Chimes toward the cook wagon. Pretty quickly a wrangler brought coffee for Horse Creek's mayor and another for J. C.

"You made time from the Red River," Deal said, looking off at his companions whom he had instructed to leave him alone with Klanghorn.

"Would've took longer, but when I got your message, we pushed. Though," he added, "I was careful not to run weight off of the beeves."

"Good thinking." Deal smiled.

"So tell me what's on your mind. Why did you want them up here soon, and now you want me to hold 'em?"

"The town's ready. But we need a couple of days. There's a stretch of track still to be laid, and the last of the loading pens. The deal will favor you."

"The boys are bustin' out all over."

"I'm not surprised."

"Heard there was trouble in Horse Creek," J. C. said, squinting at his visitor.

"Well . . ." Deal cleared his throat, looking over at his two riding companions. He had never liked venturing far out of town on a horse by himself. Especially now with the possibility of Cherokee Bill back in the country. "I did want to see if you had anybody with you named Hagstrom. Bill Hagstrom. Some people call him Cherokee Bill."

"No. I got nobody with such a name. 'Course, you know how it is. They is sometimes men with summer names. A man don't always know who he is dealing with except when it is already late." He spat at a pile of fresh horse manure. "Nope. Don't know that name."

"Big man. Built like a bull."

"We got a lot of them, and a few of them," J. C. said, and he was beginning to feel a little annoyed at the banker for stressing what appeared to him as something so unimportant, and also Deal hadn't answered him about the town.

Deal saw that he had pushed far enough, so he said quickly, "All right, then. We just wanted you to know that the town is open. You and your men are welcome. But I . . . personally would like you to wait a couple of days." And then he added, "Mr. Klanghorn, I promise I will make it well worth your while. You understand, the bank will pay you ten percent over what you get for your herd. But this is between the two of us—you and me." He watched the cattleman turning it over.

"No longer than two," Klanghorn said. He spat again, almost exactly in the same spot as a moment ago. "How about the law? I hear you got the law in town."

"News travels fast."

"Bad news always."

"I know how you're saying that, but we've got a man who's been through it all. He won't take any foolishness from anybody, that's for sure—but he don't hand it out, either. I do believe he is fair. And your ten percent is going to look good to you."

"Do you need him?" Klanghorn asked, quickly cutting his eye to Deal to catch any reaction.

"Just why we need him—for the general feeling of the town. There've been some holdups. Ryan Hollinger, our last marshal, got shot up by a gang of owl hooters. That was a while back. We figured with the herds starting to come in—" Deal stopped. He realized he had been talking too much, and he saw that J. C. Klanghorn realized it too.

"Are you laying on a marshal on account of the cattle?" J. C. said, his good eye on the banker like it was loaded. "Or on account of this feller you was asking me about?" His tone bending to more intense meaning on those last words.

Ed Deal managed a meaningless smile. He'd always had trouble with one-eyed people, never knowing which eye to look at. "Both, I'd say, but mostly on account of Hagstrom."

"Long as your man don't hamper the boys. They have rid a long trail."

"For sure."

"What's this feller's name? Who is he?"

"His name? His name is Slocum. John Slocum."

A few minutes later, when Ed Deal and his two

companions rode out of the camp, J. C. Klanghorn stood by the saddle rig looking after them.

Presently he was joined by Hendry Chimes. "When are we taking them in?" the trail boss asked.

"I told him day after tomorrow, the forenoon," J. C. said, his eyes still at the place where the three visitors had disappeared around the stand of cotton-woods.

He was still looking after the departed visitors when his trail boss left him. J. C. stood there swing-hipped, and then he reached up with his stiff thumb and pushed back the brim of his Stetson hat. His eyes were still on the cottonwoods.

"Jesus H. Christ," he muttered half aloud. He lifted his hat then, and set it down with the brim low over his brow, shading his eyes. "Shit," he said, and started walking toward the remuda to rope out his saddle pony. He was thinking how much he needed that extra money.

6

Some people had put it that Ed Deal looked exactly what he was—a banker, and at the same time an undertaker. What they must have meant was that he was always dressed in black, which set off his very white—bloodless, it seemed—skin; was thin-lipped; terse in speech; and had a mind like a diamond. Ed Deal missed nothing. He would have made a first-rate gambler. And, in fact, he was, but mostly within the bounds of his twin professions. Cards were not interesting. People were. People could be manipulated while cards—unless you were a professional mechanic who could second-deal, read marked cards, or feel shaved ones—were in fact a sap's game. You couldn't win, that is, unless you devoted yourself full-time to the profession. Deal knew that this was so in every enterprise; though, as he could see, most people didn't. Dedication was the word. And in banking he was a dedicated man. And by banking he included all money transactions, such as real estate, loans, mining stock. At the same time he had devoted much time to his career as an undertaker.   Time but not study. He was a self-appointed mortician. It had all come about from the promise he had given his dying mother: that he would follow in his father's footsteps.

And he had done so. But it was banking—that is to say, money—that had truly called him. And the manipulation of people. Power—yes. He'd figured it out. There was power in money and in advising on money matters and in withholding funds from the unworthy. Lending to those who were deserving also lent the aroma of power to the lender. And—this thought had only occurred to him in his middle years —burying the dead could be seen, too, as a sort of power. Ed Deal was a thoughtful man and he had long wondered at the thrill he often received as he gazed down into a dead face lying in his mortuary.

These thoughts and conjectures were necessarily private. Private, too, was his secret. His *great* secret, was how he put it to himself. Nobody, no one, knew it. There had been a couple of occasions when he'd almost been caught, but luck had favored him, and the two experiences had served to bolster his already tremendous caution. But his new arrangements to guard his secrecy opened the unfortunate consequences of his horsemanship. Since he had to find a place where it was unlikely that anyone would surprise him, and where there would be little chance of his being heard, it meant he had to ride a distance away from town. He was a poor horseman to say the least, which was also something he kept quite to himself. But so long as his practicing with his target shooting remained totally unknown, the sufferings he endured in the saddle—and often out of it as a result of being thrown—were worth it. So he told himself.

And so while he had spent a great deal of time and effort at his shooting practice with the definite aim of becoming first-rate at the craft, he had never had the impulse to overcome his total inability with horse-flesh.

Lending money—the bank's money, to be sure—could be most interesting. He had discovered this early on when Stefanie "Lady" Godiva had approached him for a loan to widen her business in town. In the course of the relationship between the bank and Lady Godiva—who on Deal's advice used a different name when signing the papers—the lady made money, the depositors made money, the bank made money, and of course, Ed Deal made money. He found that he was also in the favored position of reaping extra rewards for his advice, etcetera. In fact, he had insisted on this part of the arrangement. After all, as he told the lady, he would be a sorry banker if he didn't check the collateral. Which he did on a pretty regular basis. And which he was doing right now.

It was a Sunday, and the bank was closed. The shades were drawn in his office, which had an adjoining room with a wide sofa, and thick bearskin rugs on the floor. At the moment Ed Deal and Lady Godiva were lying naked on the bearskins.

"My dear, that was—as usual—perfectly delightful."

"You mean you liked it."

"I want more, in fact," he said, reaching over and playing his fingers in her soft, hairy crotch. She was soaking wet.

"God, Eddie, so do I." And she turned toward

him, lifting her leg to wrap it around his already thrust-ing hips.

"I want to be on top this time," she gasped, and he lay back while she lifted to receive his organ inside her pushing vagina.

Then she sat up on him, her back straight, one hand reaching behind to play with his balls, while she squirmed and wiggled on top of him and he thrust himself upward in frantic ecstasy.

She let go of his testicles then, and came down to rub her nipples along his mouth and licking tongue.

"My God," he gasped. "Oh, my God. Help me! Help me! God, I'm dying. I can't stand it."

While she urged him with her bucking loins, her gasps of exquisite pleasure as she rode his long post, taking it all the way up, as far as it would go, to wiggle down on it, then to raise up, teasing, and lowering herself slowly until he cried out in his madness.

"Darling—darling, please come, come, come!"

Until she, too, could bear it no longer and, finding the rhythm with him, rode him to the exploding climax.

And again they lay beside each other, exhausted, supine, and totally happy.

"My God, that's some cock you've got, Eddie."

Deal hated being called Eddie, even by Godiva, but he loved it when she complimented him on his size and prowess.

Presently he said, "This is a good place to do it, don't you think?"

"I think any place is good," she replied, tickling his ear with the tip of her tongue.

"But this is especially good."

"Well, it's certainly private and quiet."

She had started to rub her right breast with its

large, hard nipple along the side of his arm. Looking
down, her eyes gleamed as she saw his organ stirring. Then she slipped down beside him and took
him in her mouth.

Deal's penis was instantly rigid as she sucked him
slowly, tickling his shaft with her tongue as she went
up and down on him. Until finally he came again,
almost choking her—to the utter delight of both of
them.

Some while later she stirred beside him. "Why do
you like it so much here, Eddie? It's a funny place to
make love, isn't it? I mean—a bank!"

"But the point is," he said, "the point is, this is
where the money is!"

Then he lay silently on the rug beside her, thinking of how she had made love to Slocum, and still he
had not taken her up on her job offer, which origi-
nally had been his idea. But lying beside her now, he
felt the wonderful thrust of pleasure in him as he
recalled the way she'd looked when he told her that
Slocum had agreed to his offer to be marshal. By
God, he was thinking now, that was as good as sex,
maybe even better. Being ahead of her like that.

But he laughed silently at that, for while he knew
that it was in a way true—as good as sex—only not
when he had a hard-on. Ed Deal was a realist.

It didn't take Slocum long to "run into" the members
of the town council; one at a time, as he had with
Parker Tilbury and, of course, with Ed Deal. Slocum
by now had a pretty good notion about them. He'd
had to contact Ed Deal again in regard the bodies of
Bill Wellman and Jock Kramer, each having been
killed with a shotgun blast.

"That is a wicked weapon," the banker-undertaker had observed to the new marshal. He'd kept the bodies in the icehouse, which stored the two-hundred-pound blocks of ice cut from the Horse River and packed in sawdust; waiting for somebody to come forward and claim one or both. But no one did, and so the council paid for burial.

Slocum, as new marshal, got in on the tail end of it.

"They like to been cut in two," he said to Deal. "Somebody came in real close. Maybe somebody they knew."

"You're very observant, Slocum."

"Isn't that one thing I was hired for?" Slocum's tone was sour.

"Bill Hagstrom is one tough man," Deal said.

"So is the son of a bitch who killed those two men," replied the new marshal of Horse Creek.

Ed Deal's little eyes opened wide. Slocum thought he looked as though he'd just awakened from a catnap. There was surprise on his face, and then his features folded into caution.

"You don't think it was Cherokee, that it?"

"I know damn well it wasn't."

"How come?"

"Why would Hagstrom figure those two for the lynchers? Everybody knows Wellman and Kramer spoke up for Dummy. For sure, Hagstrom would have gotten that news."

"I wonder. . . ." The banker put his forefinger to the corner of his mouth, pensive. "I wonder," he repeated.

But Slocum had already walked off and left him. To the banker's great annoyance. Still, he controlled himself. It was valuable to know where the new marshal stood in regard the Wellman-Kramer killing; how he looked at things in town.

Meanwhile Slocum had walked down to the Wild Horse Eatery and ordered a coffee from Kelly Kenton. There were a few customers in the place, and so he didn't engage the girl in conversation but was content to sit quietly alone, going over the situation he was finding himself in. Nothing was clear. But he supposed that had to be expected. After all, whoever had lynched Dummy Jensen was pretty sure to be concerned with covering his tracks, or theirs. Since it was a small posse, they would have a better chance for success. But somebody wasn't very smart, or rather, somebody was getting fearful, even desperate. Otherwise, why kill the two men who had defended Dummy? Because the two men might have led someone to the lynchers? He had a pretty good idea who the lynchers were, but he needed proof. Wellman and Kramer could have contributed to that, he was sure. Their killer must have thought so too.

What was more, things were going to be a lot more difficult when the J. C. cowboys hit town. He'd have his hands more than full, and for a moment he considered the possibility of getting some deputies. But he needed men he could trust. Not easy, that.

It was clear to him that Ed Deal was running the council, if not the town, with a tight hand, and therefore was the one to watch. The man was quiet, but he penetrated everywhere. And he was feared. Most people referred to him as Mr. Deal, only the council showing any familiarity, and of course, Colonel Humboldt Smithers, who had only the other day printed the fiery editorial about Bill Wellman and

Jock Kramer, demanding to know why they had been murdered and scouting fully the notion that it was "a road agent" or someone "under the influence of the demon rum." The Colonel hadn't spelled out any names, but it was clear he was pointing to "people in high places who would prefer to keep the Dummy Jensen case closed—closed—closed!"

Strong medicine, Slocum had pointed out to his friend over a drink the day before. And he had warned him to be careful. People he knew of had been beaten and shot up for less.

But the Colonel was a stalwart. "I will not lower my flag for whoever the scum are," he had retorted stoutly. "I've an idea who they are. You know it too. No proof, you have said. True. But truth, proof, will present itself. It must!" His jowls quivering with the force of his expostulation, he had downed his drink almost at a gulp. Whereupon a coughing seizure had almost brought him to the floor. It took several minutes for him to recover so that he could start on another round.

In the Wild Horse, Slocum thought of the old man and his colorful ways and smiled to himself. He was suddenly jolted from what had become reverie when a soft voice spoke at his elbow.

"Hello, Mr. Slocum. Would you like some more coffee?"

And there she was, neat, soft, her eyes gentle and sad; yet she was smiling. Slocum felt something stir in his chest.

"You make good coffee, Kelly."

"You sound as though you were an expert," she said, and nodded good-bye to a customer who was leaving.

"I am." He grinned and pushed his cup toward her.

When she returned with it, he said, "How about supper? You remember I asked you."

He thought her face darkened slightly, but he could have been mistaken.

"I think—I think not. But thank you."

"I wasn't figuring to hit you with a lot of questions."

"I know." She looked away for a moment to see if the lone customer at the counter wanted anything, then returned her glance to him. "I know," she said again. "I—I'd just like to wait if you wouldn't mind."

"Sure. And remember what I said to you about needing help. If you ever do, remember me."

Her smile was suddenly quite open then. "I haven't forgotten, Mr. Slocum."

"Call me John."

"Mr. John," she said, suddenly teasing. "Or— Marshal John?"

"Just John." And he felt her smile drawing him right in his guts. "Maybe if you wait too long, I'll have to arrest you."

Walking away from the little café, his thoughts were full of her, and so was his body.

And then suddenly, as he found himself down by the stock pens, he had an idea. Twenty minutes later he was on his spotted pony and riding out of town. The sunlight was flooding the whole of the prairie as he headed toward Crazy Woman Creek. A name had been sticking in his memory. A name he'd overheard in the Last Drop Saloon. Chimes. Hendry Chimes. But it had eluded him.

He rode quickly as the sun filled the sky with the first warmth of the day. What were the Texans waiting for? They should be closer by now. And yet he remembered that the Colonel had said that the J.C. herd was waiting at Crazy Woman Creek. And it was he who had mentioned Hendry Chimes. Chimes. It was Kansas. Chimes. At Lawrence—with Quantrill. And suddenly Slocum felt something shoot through him like a hot iron.

The sun was hot on the lean prairie, and on Slocum and the spotted horse. He didn't push, though he had been eager to get to the J. C. camp before Klanghorn and his men started pushing the beeves into town. He didn't really know why he had been drawn to ride out to see the Texas herd and, to be sure, the Texans; only a couple of things were nagging at the edges of his mind. One, of course, was the name Chimes. But before that, the notion that Cherokee Bill might indeed try slipping into town in the wake of the excitement the herd would whip up—and the cowhands would surely sustain, at least till their money ran out —seemed to fit well. Hagstrom could slip into town, wreak his vengeance at his leisure, and slip out. Whatever he did could easily be taken as a result of the wild Texans. It made sense, then, for Slocum to meet with J. C. Klanghorn and see if there was some way to cool the raunchy cowboys a bit. But he also wanted to have a look-see at the drovers. There was also the possibility that Hagstrom might have wangled his way onto the payroll to give him a legitimacy of some kind.

Hell, he didn't know. This being a lawman was more trouble than a man could shake a stick at. He'd

had a brief spell at it in the past and hadn't cottoned
to it then. And this time he liked it even less. The
whole situation with Dummy Jensen was messy. Yet
in a sense he felt a pull toward righting what was
clearly a wrong. Only, Slocum knew himself well
enough to understand that he wasn't in the business
of doing good works. He was in the business of sur-
vival, and having a good time and a certain amount
of excitement which inevitably was part of the deal.

His thoughts centered now on Cherokee Bill Hagstrom. The man was a vicious killer—no question.
But if he was going to get him back to the sheriff of
Big Horn alive, it wasn't going to be easy. There
wasn't a doubt in his mind that Deal and his council
members would be looking to gun down Hagstrom;
they more than likely expected him to. And then
there was also the question of who the hell Hagstrom
was. He could be anybody. He could already be in
Horse Creek; could have been there for weeks for the
matter of that.

He had been riding about an hour when he suddenly felt it. The feeling in his bones, in his nerves,
that something was not right. He knew the feeling
well, had known it all his life. He sometimes called it
his "Indian feeling." For it was like them. Slocum,
like the Indians, knew how to listen to himself. And
he always minded what he heard. He knew now, just
as he knew the fingers on his hand, that somebody
had cut his trail.

The trail had narrowed now as he approached a
high cutbank. Slocum didn't lift his pace but waited
until he was abreast of a big stand of cottonwoods,
then, rounding the cutbank at the same time, he cut
off the trail and circled back, riding fast now at a

brisk canter. Suddenly he spotted a game trail leading away from the cutbank, but he cantered past it, then cut into the trees and, moving slowly now, worked deep into the cottonwoods and some aspen. He had a clear view of the trail for some distance. Dismounting, he pulled the Winchester out of its scabbard, found a natural breastworks of some fallen limbs, and, settling behind it, waited.

Colonel Humboldt Smithers was enjoying his late-morning "medicinal" as he called it. That is to say, a glass of bourbon whiskey, not purchased over the bar but poured liberally from his own private bottle in the office of the *Horse Creek Gazette*. The Colonel was feeling expansive, rather full of himself, for he had just completed another blistering editorial on the "Lynching of Olaf 'Dummy' Jensen."

By the Almighty, he was thinking, if that doesn't raise some sparks, what in the devil will! But something had to be done. Humboldt Smithers was anything but overtly sentimental; he hated sticky sentiment almost as much as he hated injustice. And it was injustice he was writing about. Injustice and the arrogance of those "stupid clowns" who had swept justice into their own hands and then dropped it into an outhouse!

Ah, he was feeling good! He reached for his glass and took another swallow. His eyes were heavy. Well, he had earned a snooze, hadn't he?

Suddenly he was wide-awake. The knock on the shaky old office door was loud, determined, even authoritative.

Without waiting for him to respond, his visitor pushed open the door and walked in.

Humboldt Smithers was sitting bolt upright in his chair, his nose wrinkling against the door that accompanied the caller into his office.

"You the head of this here newspaper?" the man asked in a demanding tone of voice, as though he was accusing him. He was dressed in filthy buckskin, his face covered with hair, his outrageous breath reaching across the room to strike the Colonel's sensitive nostrtils even more strongly as he came closer.

In a flash the Colonel's thoughts had turned to Cherokee Bill Hagstrom. Surely . . . But Humboldt Smithers hadn't survived the riverboat gambling life, the medicine-man circuit, nor the woes and throes of newspaper editorializing without having learned to keep his wits where they needed to be.

"That I am. And you, sir?"

"Just want you and your paper to know Cherokee Bill's in town," Felix said, sniggering as he thought of Bile and Lolly covering him from outside the building, and also as he watched the Colonel's face.

But his laughter dried quickly when he saw that the newspaper man was not impressed; more, he wasn't afraid.

"So . . . ?" The Colonel's eyebrows lifted elaborately as he looked down his long, bony nose at the man who had brought him this gingery headline.

"I will pass the word, sir. What else can I do for you?"

"Print it. Print it in your paper. Got that?"

"I'll print it." Humboldt spoke softly, covering his fear with arrogance, a device that had proven itself in the past and seemed to be working now. He knew full well that Cherokee Bill was no man to cross. At the same time a part of his mind was entertaining the possibility that this individual standing there, stinking up his office, might, just might be an impostor.

"'Case you don't believe I be Cherokee Bill..." the visitor said with chilling accuracy into Humboldt's thoughts, "this here can always be the convincer." And like a striking snake he had brought the Arkansas throwing knife from its scabbard at his waist.

The Colonel's cheeks worked, and he looked as though he were trying to chew his words to the right consistency before speaking. "Certainly, sir. No question as to your—identity. No question at all."

Felix was grinning, the power of the great moment washing all over the room. "Good enough, old man. Just remember that." The knife pointed at the newspaper lying on the Colonel's desk. "And remember—you be careful what you write about Cherokee Bill!"

Felix waited for it to sink in, then, holstering the wicked knife, he turned on his heel, sniffing wetly, and stomped out of the little office.

Colonel Humboldt Smithers reached for the bottle of bourbon. He was mightily relieved; especially for the fact that his visitor had not noticed the special bourbon and wanted it.

Slocum could hear the horse approaching: one rider. And in the next moment he realized that the rider was having trouble. He heard the horse nicker, and a man cursing, and then a louder, gasping curse and the drum of the horse's hooves; and the next moment the animal came rushing around the cutbank. He was riderless, his reins dragging on the ground until suddenly he stepped on them and jerked to a faltering stop.

Slocum was down on one knee, well protected by the breastwork of fallen limbs. The bay horse had stopped and now was cropping at the short buffalo grass. Slocum stood up and put his hand over his own horse's muzzle to keep him from wickering. Fortunately he was downwind of the riderless animal so that there was less chance of recognition on its part.

Meanwhile he heard a man's voice calling the horse, and finally he heard steps as he drew back deeper into the trees. He saw the small figure coming down the trail and was just bringing the man into his sights when to his astonishment he recognized who it was.

Of course, Ed Deal couldn't see the man who had him in his rifle sight, and he was too busy fuming and stomping along the uneven trail in his Wellingtons, which were too tight for him to notice much of anything.

Slocum had just reached the conclusion that the banker hadn't been necessarily following him but had been heading for somewhere or other on his own. Was it to the cattle herd? He remained motionless, still with his Winchester ready in case of any surprises, debating with himself whether or not to step out and confront Deal. But then he had a better idea.

It took some moments for the inept horseman to catch his mount, and then several moments for him to find a patch of ground with enough elevation for him to be able to get up into the saddle. The animal was obviously rented; not very good horseflesh, Slo-

cum could see, yet still with enough life in it to dump
Ed Deal.

The banker finally climbed onto the horse, and
they started off at a fast walk. Slocum waited a few
minutes more and then mounted his spotted pony and
followed.

It didn't take long for him to find out what Deal
was up to. The banker rode for about another half
hour and stopped near some cottonwoods and box
elders alongside a creek, not very far from Crazy
Woman Creek where the Klanghorn beeves were
supposed to be waiting.

Slocum remained hidden near the lip of a draw
while Deal dismounted, set up some targets against
some trees, and started firing away. To Slocum's astonishment he realized that the man was good. In
fact, he was damn good. At target shooting. Real
shooting—in a gunfight—would be quite another
matter. He could tell that. But with the targets, Deal
was accurate almost every time.

Slocum didn't stay long watching the display. As
he rode away he wondered why the banker was practicing. Was he expecting the need to protect himself?
Or was it some sort of sport for him? Hard to say,
and he had no intention of asking. Not now, at any
rate.

It was just past the middle of the forenoon when
he topped a slight rise and looked down at Crazy
Woman Creek and the J. C. herd bunched there with
men holding them. It looked as though someone was
giving orders down there. And almost directly he
saw a rider walk his horse toward some grazing
steers; his calling to them followed by the pop of the
end of his lariat rope that he cracked over their heads

and rumps, cutting up to where Slocum sat his pony. Cattle began to hump up onto their feet and started moving in the direction in which more cowboys were hazing them. Some of the steers were objecting and acting pretty feisty, but they were soon worried into the building herd as the bawling increased and the dust rose from the dry ground.

Slocum loosened the thong on his Colt and now kicked the spotted pony into a brisk canter as he started down the slope toward the moving cattle. Already he spotted the man standing by the chuck wagon watching him. A big man, lean, and, it seemed even from this distance, with knobby limbs.

Down by the chuck wagon, J. C. Klanghorn squinted up at the sun, then lowered his good eye to the approaching rider.

"Know him?" Hendry Chimes said, riding up on the big steel-dust gelding.

J. C. spat at a loose clump of sage, then reached to his shirt pocket and brought out the makings. For a moment he held the tobacco sack and papers in his two hands and let his good eye roam over the herd that was just starting to move.

"I know him," he said, and started to build his smoke.

"Texas?" The trail boss was a big man with big hands and a very wide face. His eyes were on the approaching rider as he spoke.

"Texas and everywheres," J. C. Klanghorn said.

His trail boss turned his head now and watched the quick movements of the other man's fingers as he poured just the right amount of tobacco into the paper, pulled the string on the sack with his teeth to close it, slipped it into his shirt pocket, then with both hands rolled the cigarette, and in one swift stroke licked it over his tongue and rolled it tight, twisting the end. In the same flow of movement he struck a match on the back of his thigh and canted his head to the flame.

"I wonder what the hell he is doing here, then?" Chimes said.

"You know him, do you?" J. C. also had kept his eye on the rider.

"Dunno. Might." Hendry Chimes came down from his horse. "He got a handle, has he?"

"Slocum," the cattleman said. "John Slocum." He was watching the side of his trail boss's face, and then he said again, "You reckon you know who he is?"

"I dunno," Hendry Chimes said.

But J. C. Klanghorn saw his hand drop in the direction of his holstered six-gun, and in a moment his hand was resting right on it.

As John Slocum rode up to where they were standing.

7

There was nothing small about Cherokee Bill Hagstrom. Even as a lad he was big. Especially his nose. In fact, early on, he'd acquired the nickname Big Nose Bill. It was a common name in the mountain country where Bill had first appeared. And, in fact, several men wore their big noses like a badge in the north country. Bill, however, had tried to hide his nose at first. As a boy, he had taken to covering his face with a big red bandanna. But this only drew even more attention to the size of his nose. Finally, being a big boy, he began to take the opposite view, which was that his nose was an emblem of distinction. Oddly, not so long later in his young life, he found further use for the bandanna. It was nifty for disguising him when he was engaged in the pursuit of his livelihood. William, as his mother had called him, soon became Bill; and Bill soon turned into Cherokee Bill. This transformation occurred when he was quite young and killed his first man—a half-blood Cherokee. For some quaint reason or other the name Cherokee attached itself to Bill.

In the idiom of the day, Cherokee Bill became known as a man from two miles north of hell who'd never moved away. He weighed more than two hundred pounds and was well over six feet tall. He towered above his fellows.

Cherokee's initial appearance in Horse Creek some years back had been memorable and quite in keeping with his character. It had taken place in a saloon.

According to Colonel Humboldt Smithers, who was Slocum's principal—indeed, only—informant on the life and character of Cherokee Bill, the man with the big nose had paused in one of the Horse Creek saloons for refreshment.

As the Colonel described it in his vivid speech, the giant, "with the outlandish proboscis" had leaned against the bar "as a giant pine leans against an outcropping and was casually examining his surroundings. In those days, at least, his face was virtually hidden in a mask of black whiskers which forbade close scrutiny." Apparently at some point Cherokee found something amusing in the scene he was surveying, for he trumpeted a roar of laughter. A man standing farther down the bar heard the sound, turned and approached Cherokee, and slammed him genially on the back.

"By Gar, Bill, I ain't seen you in this good while," he'd shouted. "Where you bin?"

The Colonel had made a gesture with his hand. "Cherokee said nothing, just waved his big paw in the general direction of the Continental Divide. The other man began to tell him about some gamblers who had been held up over on the other side of Mosquito Pass; three gamblers who'd been stripped of two thousand dollars."

The Colonel had paused. "Mind you, this is hearsay, but it is good copy. I ran the story some years back in my column, which dealt with the more colorful aspects of our town and which I customarily headed with the delightful title, 'Breakfast Bullets.'" He paused to chuckle and then swept on. "To make the point more quickly, the three gamblers made it to Horse Creek, one with frozen feet, who shortly died, while the other two were standing right in the saloon at that moment. The short of it was, one of them came over to where Bill was standing and made the fatal mistake of saying he was pretty damn sure he'd seen him somewhere not too long ago."

Humboldt took a quick drink and resumed. "Quicker'n a cat can lick his ass, Cherokee put down his drink and grabbed the gambler by the ear. And when he hit the man, it's been told that the blow could be heard above the tremendous noise of the saloon. The man just flew across the room, taking chairs, tables, and people with him.

"'Sorry, boys,' Cherokee says as he walks toward the swinging doors. 'I just don't like a man that's been robbed telling that he's maybe seen me somewheres.'"

Slocum was remembering the story as he rode down the long slope toward the J. C. herd and the two men standing by the chuck wagon. He had wondered aloud to the Colonel why no one said that they could identify Cherokee Bill, since he hadn't been wearing any mask or bandanna when he'd first come to Horse Creek. But the Colonel reminded him that, no, while he hadn't any bandanna on his face, he was covered with his thick black whiskers. Which, it was reported, he had long ago shaved. And Humboldt Smithers had added, "There is no way anybody—I mean, anyone—can know what Cherokee looks like." And then he had further added, "And if there should be, there is no one—no body—who would have the guts to say so. Surely not, after what happened to that gambler and God knows how many others. That man's neck and jaw were broken. With one punch! A single punch, mind you! It is unnecessary for me to add that the gambler ended up quite dead."

Slocum had half his attention on his horse's ears as he rode up to where J. C. Klanghorn and his trail boss were standing. The spotted pony had often shown himself to be a sensitive animal; more so than usual for a horse. And Slocum, being a man who listened to animals—especially the horses he rode, as he also listened to the land, the weather, the sky —listened now. The spotted pony was feeling spooked about something. He wasn't just walking any longer but stepping, lifting his legs higher than he usually did, with his neck arched, while his ears moved—now out to the sides, now forward, but not yet back. Slocum knew the signs well—up and forward simply meant a keen listening on the part of the animal, while sideways indicated caution, even fear. When the ears were laid back, watch out—don't get near those hooves or teeth. Mostly now as Slocum got closer to the two men, the ears were out sideways.

J. C. Klanghorn was the first to speak. "What kin I do for you, mister?"

"I am looking for J. C. Klanghorn," Slocum said, coming closer to himself in his saddle. He still had some attention on his horse's ears, and now, when the animal snorted and started to spook, he took up his reins.

And in the next instant his hand had swept to his holstered Colt and drawn in a streak—so fast, it was as though the gun had simply appeared in his hand—and shot the head off the rattler that had appeared right at the spotted pony's feet.

"'Preciate that, mister," J. C. Klanghorn said, sober as a Sunday preacher. "Suspicioned something not right when I seen your pony's ears."

The smile on the other man's face was as tight as a stretched piece of pigging string.

"I be Klanghorn."

"Slocum. John Slocum." And he watched how they took that.

Klanghorn simply nodded, while his companion stared hard at him.

"Whyn't you step down," Klanghorn said. "We're fixin' to start the herd into town. I hear you're the new marshal."

Slocum still wasn't wearing a star, much to Deal's objection, and also to his associates' on the council. But Slocum preferred not to. He had his reasons. "That tin makes a good target," he'd said. And that was that.

He swung down from his horse as Klanghorn turned to his trail boss, saying, "Get 'em moving, Hendry." And then he cut his eye quickly to Slocum.

Slocum was watching the trail boss who was looking right at him. There was something like a sneer behind his face, but it was buried.

"This here is my trail boss," Klanghorn said suddenly, signaling to Cookie, who was fussing around the chuck wagon. "You'll take some arbuckle, will you?"

"Sure will," Slocum said.

And then J. C. remembered he hadn't finished what he'd started to say to his visitor. "Chimes. Hendry Chimes," he said.

Slocum stood quite still, matching the other man's look. Suddenly the man named Hendry Chimes spoke.

"Heard you rode with Quantrill, Slocum."

"A man can hear a lot of things," Slocum said, suddenly coming together fast.

"That's the kind of thing a man remembers," Chimes said. "I was there. I was at Lawrence."

"What's your real name?" Slocum said. He felt Klanghorn tighten beside him and caught the burning in the trail boss's eyes.

"You like funnin', do you?"

"Take it slow, Hendry," Klanghorn said, swiftly cutting in. "May be some mistake here."

"No mistake," Slocum said. "But I can let it pass if you like, Klanghorn. Excepting I am the law in this here country."

"I kin handle him, J. C."

"No!" Klanghorn had stepped between them.

"I'm the law here, Klanghorn," Slocum said.

"I'd like you to tell me what you mean, Marshal." J. C. was holding his temper with difficulty.

"I mean this man here is not Hendry Chimes."

"How do you know that?"

"There weren't two Hendry Chimes at Lawrence. Only the one."

"That's what I just got through telling you," snapped Chimes.

"Then you're lying."

Klanghorn took a step between them, holding up his hands. "I want to know what you two men are fighting about. Slocum, why do you say he isn't what he says he is? That's what I want to know!"

"There was only one Hendry Chimes with Quantrill, and it is not this man."

"How do you know that?"

"Chimes is dead."

"How do you know that?"

"I know because I killed him."

"Well, it sure as hell beats working the wolves," Felix was saying to his two companions as they sat around their camp fire, some distance north of Horse Creek.

His two companions could only agree. They had struck again, twice, each one taking his turn at being Cherokee Bill. Their frightened prey had been only too glad to divvy up.

"But shouldn't we ought to be heading north now?" Lolly asked. "Shit, Felix, we hang about too long, we're chancing it to get our ass caught."

"Go where?" Felix had snarled as he picked his teeth with a piece of buffalo bone.

"Montana," Bile said. "That's where the wolves are now."

"I don't reckon so. By the time we get there, every son of a bitch wolfer in the West will of bin there first," Felix said. "Hell, look how it was here. Shit, I recollect when this here country was a sea of buffalo; just ike a fucking ocean, was how some said it. Millions, thousands of buffalo."

"And wolves," added Lolly.

"'Course, you stupid asshole. That is what I am talking about."

They fell silent, each turning it over in his own thoughts.

The wolves, as everybody knew, followed the buffalo herds. The number roaming the plains was incredible. They had been greatly increased by the thousands of skinned buffalo carcasses left by the hide hunters to rot. The wolves liked the meat, particularly the stench. After filling themselves until they were not even able to stand, they rolled joyfully in the decaying meat. This feeding and rich perfuming led to much breeding, and they raised large families.

The wolfer had his work cut out. The best wolf hunting had been until recently in the southern plains region of western Kansas; but with the buffalo herd dwindling to near extinction, the northern region, especially in central Montana, along the Milk and Musselshell Rivers, became popular. But even here the end was in sight. And it was this bitter, brute fact that was occupying Felix, Bile, and Lolly as they contemplated their future. Presently, well off the beaten track due to the necessity of escaping the clutches of at least two posses, they realized that it was a brute gamble if they moved north to search for wolves. The country up there, as each pointed out to the other two again and again—and they loved to repeat themselves—was undoubtedly hunted out and likely overrun with wolfers who, everyone knew when there would be no wolves to kill, would turn to killing each other.

"We would be dumb-ass buggers to head north," Felix said as he reached over to poke the fire. "Shit, we could try some stock lifting, excepting the god-damn vigilantes is all burred up around this part of the country. Shit . . ."

They sat now in huddled, glum silence. Their camp consisted of the fire and a place to throw their blankets, which they had done already. They were used to the rough life and didn't expect anything else.

"There ain't no other wolfers 'round this here country," Felix pointed out suddenly.

"And there ain't no wolves anymore, neither," Lolly said.

"Right enough. But there is those scared-shitless fellers in the town there. I say we make one more hit and then head west. We get up into the Oregon country, we'll likely manage some better, I'll allow. 'Course, we'll hit Denver for some fun first thing."

"But we got to think about that new marshal. He is no man to mess with." Bile was sucking his teeth vigorously as he finished this declaration.

"We can handle the son of a bitch."

"Like in that saloon?" Lolly said. And the next thing he knew, he was flat on his back, feeling like his head had been split in two.

Felix stood over him with a rifle in his hand. He had struck Lolly with the barrel along the side of his head. "You watch your fucking mouth, Lolly. Next time I won't go so easy on you!"

"Jesus, Felix, you like to kilt him," Bile said. "Not that the bugger didn't deserve it," he added quickly as he noted the look in his partner's eye. "But, shit, we got to hang together," he pointed out. "We are only us down here in this goddamn place."

This was the one point on which the three could see eye to eye. They were indeed alone in this foreign and hostile country.

"You buggers watch yer mouths," Felix said, and he tossed the rifle onto his bedding. "I am the one who thought up this idea on how to make us some money when there was no way. No way at all for us to make a decent living, like any God-fearing man, so help me, God." And he turned his eyes toward the sky, wondering if he smelled rain.

"So it was you," Chimes was saying. "I reckon I've been wondering that for a long time. I'd heard a lawman back-shot him."

"It wasn't the law," Slocum said, grinding his words some to get through the hard body of the man facing him. "It was a fair fight. He drew on me."

"He was my brother," Chimes said.

"I don't care if he was your father; he drew on me. You aiming to push it, mister?"

"Not with the law."

"You wouldn't be going up against the law," Slocum said. "You'd be going against John Slocum."

The tableau had frozen into the terse, cryptic statements after Chimes had announced that he was Hendry Chimes's brother and had taken his first name for his own.

But now J. C. spoke up again. "I need my trail boss, Slocum. Why don't you settle this after we ship."

"I am in no hurry," Slocum said. He stood there, ready, right on the edge of it.

Chimes was still with it, his eyes hard on Slocum, his hand not far from his six-gun.

"Hendry..." Klanghorn's voice was cautionary. "Don't be foolish now."

"I will see you later, Slocum. Meanwhile keep clear of me."

"I will be wherever I am," Slocum said. "It will be you to keep clear of me, mister."

He let it sink into the hard man, who stood squarely in front of him. Chimes wasn't giving anything. But now he stood away, waited a moment, and then turned toward his steel-dust gelding and swiftly mounted. Without another look at either Slocum or Klanghorn, he kicked his horse into a fast canter. In a moment they heard him barking orders to the men.

"I'd like that coffee now, Klanghorn."

J. C. looked as though he were trying to suck on a lemon. He said nothing, only turned and walked toward the chuck wagon where Cookie had been standing watching the drama that had just transpired.

"Why have you been holding your herd?" Slocum asked as they squatted near the rear of the wagon and J. C. drew idly in the dirt with a stem of some sage he'd picked up.

"Thought to bring 'em in with a little feed on their bones. Makes a better look for the buyer." And the stockman cut his good eye to Slocum.

"I see." Slocum didn't believe it, and he knew Klanghorn knew he didn't. But nothing further was said on that matter.

Slocum said, "The town will be glad to have you, Klanghorn, and your men. Only all guns got to be handed in at my office or the nearest saloon. They can be picked up when the boys are done with their good times."

"Fair enough," Klanghorn said with a slow nod. "I do say the boys are pretty feisty right now."

"Got to expect it. It's a long drive from Texas."

And they both had a short chuckle on that.

"You ever run into a feller name of Cherokee Bill Hagstrom?" Slocum asked, and he let his gaze move casually to the horizon where a single cloud seemed to be standing absolutely still.

"Can't say I have." The cattleman's words were spoken to the smoke he was building in his leathery fingers. "You looking for him special?"

"I am."

"I'll keep an eye out for you."

"You mind if I take a look about?"

"You think he might be one of my men?"

"Do you know your men all that well?"

Klanghorn one-handedly struck a match on his thumbnail. "Help yourself," he said, and bent his head to the flame.

Slocum studied that a minute, wondering if he heard sincerity all the way through. He wasn't sure. But there was still something funny about Hendry Chimes suddenly coming back into his life. The Hendry he had known had ridden with Bloody Bill, had been one of Anderson's most eager killers. If his brother, who had taken his name, was even half as brutal, there could be trouble ahead when the boys hit town. And the fact that he had taken his brother's name seemed to underline that. The present Hendry Chimes looked to be as tough, as ornery, as wicked as his brother had been. Something else to look forward to, Slocum told himself wryly as he started his ride around the Klanghorn herd. Nor had he forgotten that Cherokee Bill Hagstrom had also ridden with Bloody Bill.

The Town Council was not in a happy mood as Ed Deal reported to them on the Klanghorn herd. The visitations of Cherokee Bill had shaken them all. True, they were not certain whether it was actually Cherokee Bill in person, or the man who had been throwing dice in the Last Drop with Burgess, or possibly some part of Cherokee's gang, if he had one. Nevertheless, whoever it was had shaken them plenty. By now the rest of the council had been visited, with the exception of Deal. But Cherokee had also called on some other townspeople. Tim Wernerhorn and Phil Nimrod, both of them oldsters without much to give, but easy pickings for the bandit.

"I expect I will be called on any night now," Ed Deal said sourly. "But we should be happy that Nimrod and Wernerhorn have been victimized, for it shows Hagstrom doesn't know exactly who was involved with our—uh—dispensation of justice. He's throwing buckshot and, of course, has aimed principally at the council."

"But what about Slocum?" asked Tod Ollenburgh. "Ain't he the mashal? We got to get him turned on to this. But where the hell is he?"

"He is out checking the Klanghorn herd," Deal said. "Boys, don't worry about it. Slocum's handling his job. He's making sure the J. C. men don't take this town apart."

"Good enough," Clem Dunstan said gravely. "But what about these men holding us up, taking money at

gunpoint! One of these times someone's going to get
shot up!"

"Slocum should be back anytime now, judging on
how long he's been gone," Deal said. "I'll talk to
him, get him on to this. But remember..." And
leaning on the table with one elbow he pointed his
forefinger at the group. "Remember, we do not want
him getting too close on certain things."

This brought the group to a stiff silence. Deal allowed the moment to lengthen before he spoke again.

"Don't forget, either, the reason I told Klanghorn
to hold back on bringing the herd in right away. We
want those cowboys climbing wild when they hit
town. We want them really to bust loose. You remember that!"

"Sure do," Parker Tilbury said. "I'm not too sure
why, Ed. But I reckon you got your reasons."

"I told you." There was just a necessary touch of
impatience that Ed Deal allowed in his tone as he
answered Tilbury.

"Jesus," exclaimed John Bettman. "Parker, we
went through the whole business of raunching up the
town, letting the drovers even tree it, so's with
everything angried up the committee could take
over."

"The vigilantes, you're saying," put in Parker Tilbury.

"The law," Ed Deal said firmly. "The point is, if
there's enough chaos, fear, just goddamn trouble and
shooting and a few killings—not too many!—then
the town will turn to us. They'll turn to the council,
the law, and they'll forget all about that other, the
Dummy Jensen thing."

"But what about Cherokee Hagstrom?"

"That's what we've got Slocum for."

"And what about Slocum?" Parker Tilbury asked slyly.

"He can be taken care of when his job is done. Any problem meanwhile—it's his problem. He's the marshal. We—we . . ." Ed Deal placed his fingers carefully on his chest, the soul of innocence. "We are but humble servants. . . ."

A chuckle started in the group, like a trickle of water, and it spread to another, then another, until it went around the circle and the boys were laughing, almost but not quite roaring with goodwill and laughter as their fears vanished and they felt really good. Ed Deal wasn't laughing. He was the only one not laughing. He was watching them. He was smiling.

8

He could see right off that Klanghorn and Chimes had a well road-broke herd. He spotted a few unbranded cattle and some with a brand other than the J. C. trail brand, but this was to be expected. Slocum knew very well that a trail boss who didn't reach his destination with an equal, or greater, number of cattle than he started with was considered incompetent. It was a rule that all stray unbranded cattle along the route were picked up. At times ranchers living along the trails complained angrily and became even hostile about their cattle being driven away by the trail drivers. A herd would often be stopped by these stockmen, and all the beeves not bearing the trail-brand would be taken from the drive.

The point was that a few extra cattle were always needed, especially in the Indian Territory where the Indians were always demanding "who-how" beef, as a levy for passing through their land. Of course, the trail boss would prefer giving up unbranded stock, or beef with a brand other than the trail brand. Custom had made it so.

There were some fifteen men in the Klanghorn outfit, and as far as Slocum could tell, they were fair to top hands. And Hendry Chimes was a fair hand himself, though Slocum had seen more than a few better. J. C., on the other hand, was for sure a top hand, but he was taking it easy some, Slocum noted. Sometimes when he took a quick look at the cattleman, he saw something in him, about him, that made him wonder if maybe he'd been stove up from busting too many broncs. Except why would J. C. Klanghorn be topping out broncs when he was running a spread? Well, maybe times had come hard and he'd had to turn his hand to other work. Bronc stomping was good pay if you could stand the broken bones. But the man was no longer young, and Slocum wondered if he was maybe up against it.

As he rode around the herd, some of the men nodded; some even exchanged a word of greeting; some were silent, keeping their eyes averted. But there was no one who could even suggest a fit with what he knew about Cherokee Bill.

When he dropped back to the drag, he found Klanghorn on the edge of the big dust cloud thrown up by the cattle.

"Find anything?" the cattleman asked, canting his head so that he could get his good eye right onto Slocum.

"Only that you got a well-broke herd, and they appear to be in good shape."

"We didn't push them, except at first when we made thirty miles a day, so's at night they'd be good and tired and not give trouble. But then when they got to be road-broke, we slackened off to fifteen, sixteen miles a day. Like that."

"I do believe you'll get top price for them," Slocum said.

"No sign of that one you been looking for," Klanghorn said.

"Nothing." Slocum took out a quirly and lit it. He was thinking of Hendry Chimes. "Like to ask you something." he said.

"I'm listening." The rancher was astride a big sorrel gelding. Now he leaned forward in his stock saddle and leaned his crossed forearms on the worn saddle horn.

"How long have you known Chimes?"

The cattleman pursed his lips, reached up and rubbed his forehead with the palm of his hand. "You askin' as lawman? Or personal?"

"As marshal of Horse Creek," Slocum said.

J. C. Klanghorn's good eye dropped down to Slocum's hickory shirt, to the place where a tin badge would have been.

"I have been told that the marshal's name is Slocum," he said. "But that don't mean you are him."

"It don't mean I am not, neither," Slocum said evenly, his eyes directly on Klanghorn. "But I believe you can decide that."

J. C. reached to his shirt pocket for his makings. "What do you want to know?"

"What you can tell me, providing you know, 'course."

"I don't know anything about him," Klanghorn said. "He worked for the Double R outfit down in the panhandle, for Drury Bitten. But maybe he didn't, for the matter of that. I just got that word. Now you mention it, I don't know a thing about him. He can handle the cattle and the men, and he hasn't caused me any grief. All I can say."

"Then you know nothing. Where he came from? Ever heard of his brother?"

Klanghorn shook his head. "Only when you mentioned him." And then he added, "I do see he is fast with a gun. And accurate. I figure him for a man not to argue with. But he does what I tell him."

Slocum grinned at that, his eyes looking right into that leathery face. "I do believe that, J. C. I don't figure you for a man to argue with, neither."

"They should be here sometime tomorrow," Deal was saying to Godiva, who was slowly putting her clothes back on, following one of their Sunday sessions in the bank. His indolent gaze followed her movements with an attention that was quite passive. After all, they had exercised themselves well and were ready for a little rest. Even conversation.

Deal, of course, realized full well the value of this particular pipeline, which Godiva maintained for him. The most amazing things were related in her upstairs rooms at the Three Aces. Men, under the pressure of desire, and the goodwill of satiation, revealed the most extraordinary tidbits which, when carefully pieced together by an objective individual such as Godiva, and especially Ed Deal, often made quite a tapestry. Deal could fully boast that he knew more about the denizens of Horse Creek than any ten other men put together, and moreover, more about certain husbands than their wives could possibly dream of. The connection with Godiva was a gold mine. He could have made a fortune easily here, simply by threatening, by withholding, by imputation. But Ed Deal had bigger aims than mere black-mail could offer him.

He had it on most reliable authority that there was the sure likelihood that not only was the Union Pacific planning to spread its tracks more and more through the country, but also that the latest reports on the mining possibilities around Crazy Woman Gulch were tantalizingly favorable. Already sound extracts of ore had been produced at Crazy Woman, but now it was reported that a major vein had been struck. So far this was not known to the public. It had come to Deal through the usual trustworthy channels: the bed-room of one of Godiva's girls had yielded the bulletin.

Ed was overjoyed, for it fitted in with his takeover plans for the town. Quietly, using various names, he had been buying up real estate these past two years.

"My dear, how would you like to suffer under the heavy burden of massive wealth?" he asked the love of his life as she pulled on her stockings over the most marvelous pair of legs he'd ever seen.

Godiva smiled, biting her lower lip gently as her eyes felt over his face, then lowered to his neck, his chest.

He was about to say something when there came a sudden thumping on the outside door.

Deal gave a start, then quickly took out his pocket watch and looked at it. "My dear, your company has been so enjoyable, I'd lost track of the time. I have a vital meeting to attend to right now. Will you mind?"

She had finished dressing and now rose, smiling at him through her pouting lips, a long tease that he felt all the way through him.

As the knocking came again.

"Eddie, I'll be thinking of you."

"You'd better go out the other way."

"But of course." And suddenly her eyes opened wide. There was a quite different tone in her voice as she said, "Eddie, I don't want the people of this town to see me with you, any more than you want them to see you with me. You got that—honey?" And she laid right into the last word.

Deal felt something stab his guts and cursed himself for not being more careful. She was too valuable to antagonize. He had done so before, and he had regretted it. Nor was it only a question of her withdrawn favors; there was the terrible danger and risk from her knowing so much about his plans. Once again he realized with a funny feeling inside him that she was the only one who did know.

He planted a smile on his face as he ushered her out the back door and then straightened his face to a more grave expression as he walked quickly to answer the insistent knocking. Yes, he would have to be much more careful now, with things coming to a climax. There was too much at stake to risk her anger or to endanger what he had asked her to engage in regarding John Slocum. He wanted to know what the man was up to, what he was doing, what he was thinking. Slocum had confided nothing to him thus far, and he didn't like that. Ed Deal was a man who always wanted to know where he was. Yes, he was a gambling man, but he was also a professional, a gambler who gambled with the odds heavily in his favor. It was the only way.

And he was fully composed as he unlocked the side door of the bank to admit Parker Tilbury, who was standing there waiting alone.

"You are early," Deal said, though not unpleasantly, as he led his associate inside the bank and told him to pour himself a drink and wait until the rest of the council appeared.

"Didn't realize I was all that early, Ed," Parker said with a friendly laugh.

"It is just as bad to be early for an appointment as it is to be late," Ed Deal said coolly as he walked out of the room, leaving his associate to sweat a little.

He was a stringy man with a mobile face, knobby hands, and bright brown eyes. Tom Kenton. Horse Creek's blacksmith. There was power in that stringy body, in those knobby fingers.

Slocum stood watching him finish the last shoe on the strawberry roan. Kenton worked fast, sure, humming lightly to himself as he worked—hammering in the nails, clinching them, then cutting the excess. Buffing and oiling the hoof. Now and again saying a word to the roan, who was standing well but now and again had to move against a random deerfly.

Finally he set the leg down and stood up rubbing the back of his neck with his calloused palm.

"What can I do for you, Marshal?" he said, looking at Slocum out of those bright eyes. He was wearing a peaked cap with the bill bent in a V shape. It fit his head snugly. Slocum wondered if he'd always been a blacksmith.

"I wanted to talk to you, Mr. Kenton."

"About Norah?" The words came out fast, as though he might have been afraid of his voice cracking and wanted to get it said. Yet Slocum could see this wasn't really so, for Tom Kenton was clearly a man who could hold his feelings.

"About Dummy Jensen," Slocum said.

"We'll go inside," Kenton said, leading the way toward the door of the cabin in which he and his daughter Kelly lived.

"I'll wrangle the jawbreaker," he said. "Since Kelly's to work."

And Slocum could tell the man had been a trail rider, maybe even had worked the whole thing in his time. Funny how the language, the words, never left a man. And a good thing it was, he decided as he sat down in the chair in the tiny kitchen.

"I am trying to get a picture of the town and what happened to young Jensen," Slocum said. "So I hope you don't mind me talking a bit, asking you some questions."

"I mind nothing but my own business," Kenton said, and he nodded after his words. "About all a man ought to be doing is how I figure it."

Slocum grinned at that. He liked a man who staked out his turf without any ifs or buts. "Can you tell me anything about Dummy Jensen? What was he like, did you know him at all?"

Kenton had taken a corncob pipe out of his pocket and was tamping down the tobacco in its bowl with his middle finger.

"No, nobody really knew Dummy, I'd say. Except Norah—some. She was kind to him. The boy couldn't speak, just grunt, and they say he was deaf as a barn door. See, Norah used to teach school."

He stopped, and Slocum looked away for a moment to let him have himself alone.

Tom Kenton's voice was even as he quickly resumed. "So she tried teaching him some things. 'Course, Dummy couldn't work with the class, so she worked with him alone. Did that for a couple years. I expect the boy appreciated it."

"I'd sure think so," Slocum said.

"She used to draw pictures with him. Like that. And they made up a sign language of their own. I seen 'em at it. Got so they could talk real fast." He nodded his head. "He was a good boy. Not dumb at all, he was a smart lad."

"But the posse decided he'd be the one to string up."

"I told 'em what I thought. But they didn't listen. The damn fools. Judging like that. Who the hell do they think they are?"

"Then do you know who did actually hang him?"

Kenton was already shaking his head. "Nope. I wasn't there. When I say I spoke to them, I mean I spoke to the crowd that was gathered out there in the street. Everybody was all whipped up, rarin' to wreak vengeance. The damn fools. I told 'em I didn't figure Dummy'd be able to do a thing . . . like that. But—" He stopped, shrugged, spread his arms apart slightly, still holding his pipe in one hand. "Who knows? Maybe he did. Somebody said he confessed, but how the hell a deaf and dumb boy can confess to anything, I dunno. I think they lynched him, but I—I don't want to talk about it anymore, mister."

"Good enough," Slocum said softly. He could see that the hard frown on the other man's face was there in order to hold in the sudden push of his terrible sorrow.

He stood up. "I dunno, but what you make as good coffee as your daughter does, Mr. Kenton, down at the eatery."

This brought a slow grin to the older man's face as he walked Slocum to the door.

"Any way I can help you, Marshal. I'll be glad."

For a moment it crossed Slocum's mind to ask Kenton if he'd be game for taking on as a deputy. But he decided no, the man had enough to deal with in his life without putting him in a position where it could all be opened up again.

With a nod he turned now and started down the street. But Tom Kenton's voice—firm, sure again—caught him. "I meant that, Slocum, if I can help you in any way." And then he added. "The town needs it."

Slocum had stopped, and now he turned back. He wasn't far from where the blacksmith was standing, but his quiet words carried to him.

"Maybe you can give me a handle on Ed Deal," he said. "I get the picture he like to runs this town."

A wry grin accompanied Tom Kenton's reply. "I'd say that is for sure, Marshal."

"I've met up with the council members, and I've moseyed around trying to get a hold of something on this thing that happened to Dummy and the fact that he was Bill Hagstrom's brother."

Tom Kenton nodded, taking the pipe out of his mouth. "I did hear of that too. A lot of people are scared stiff on account of that. I am not wasting a thing on them."

"What I am saying," said Slocum, "just between us, is that there is going to be one helluva lot of action going on when that herd hits town—the drovers, the possible visit from Cherokee, the whole outfit here is going to be standing on its head. Will Cherokee come in and start throwing lead, or cutting

—which he favors, by the way? Will the trail hands take the town apart? I have somehow got the feeling, Kenton, that somebody is going to be making some hay out of this pile."

"I am figuring that right along with you, Slocum. You got deputies?"

"Not a one."

"I'll side you."

Kenton's offer came immediately on Slocum's words, so fast that he felt a little shock run through him. But he also felt good.

"I do appreciate that, Kenton. I'd like to hold it in mind—a hour or two," he added with a wry grin. "See, I'll be setting up."

The blacksmith nodded. "I think you're right on Deal," he said. "I feel you're reaching to something about that man. He's a slicker—no question. He does a lot of living on those tight sleeves of his."

Slocum grinned at the reference to both Deal's whipcord body and tight-fitting clothing and his likely propensity for double-dealing or harboring an ace or two on his person. He nodded then and, turning, walked off down the street. But he was remembering that when he'd watched Ed Deal practicing at his portable target range, the mayor was wearing a fairly loose-fitting black broadcloth coat.

On an impulse he stopped in at the Wild Horse Eatery, but to his surprise and disappointment, Kelly wasn't there. He'd gotten so used to thinking of her in that place, working those long hours, that to discover her absence was a shock.

His second impulse brought him through the batwing doors of the Three Aces. Wendy was on his mind, but again fate stepped in. Wendy was busy, obviously with a customer. That left only one other way, which appeared through the enormous person of Oren the bartender.

"Godiva's been sending out that she wants to see you," the big man said as Slocum moved up to the bar. His voice carried right into Slocum's ear, even though he hadn't moved his lips a hair's breadth. Slocum admired that kind of technique, realizing that it was in such small details that the fate of a whole deal would hinge. Very often, at any rate. Such things as motionless communication; the posture a man took at the bar, which would decide how quickly he could reach his gun; how he walked down a street near the outer edge of the walk in case someone tried an attack from one of the many alleys or sides of buildings. Details. But it was details that decided on the quick and the dead. More often than not.

He didn't hurry. He nursed the beer he'd ordered, and he could feel Oren getting more and more nervous on the other side of the bar. The fat man wiped over the mahogany a number of times, obviously concerned that Slocum wasn't in any hurry to see Lady Godiva. And Slocum realized the full extent of the fear that Godiva—and very likely Deal, in cohoots with her—exerted on not only Oren but others in town. Deal, of course, had the money and political power. Godiva held a different kind of power—not so much power of the purse as power of the pussy. And so he drank his beer slowly, playing his cards in his own time.

The big man was watching him, but he was being careful not to push, obviously remembering what had happened not so long ago when he'd tried to send

Wendy on her way. Slocum was wondering who would appear first—Wendy or Godiva. And he was enjoying himself. When he finished his beer, he felt Oren watching him closely to see what he would do. And when he ordered another beer, he thought the bartender would say something. But just at that moment the door to the back room opened and Lady Godiva emerged.

She caught his eyes on her right away and, with a smile, walked slowly toward him. Slocum didn't miss a single undulation of that fabulous body. And yet the sexuality of her movement wasn't the least obvious. It was as though her animality lay just below the surface of her skin, moving through her like breath. Slocum felt his erection pulsing against his taut trousers like a tent pole.

She came in close, her smile mostly in her lips, and when she was standing beside him, Oren placed a glass on the bar.

"Join me?" she said, her eyes still holding Slocum's.

"I prefer to drink privately when I'm with company," he said, picking up both glasses and moving toward one of the free tables.

She smelled of musk as with his foot he hooked a chair leg and drew the chair out from the table so she could sit. He took a deep breath.

"You like it, Slocum?"

"On you it's good."

He sat down.

"We could go to my room, or do you prefer it out here?"

"Business first."

"Business?"

"Oren said you were looking for me."

"Does that mean business?"

"Dear, you're a beautiful thing, and I love to screw with you, but I wasn't born this morning."

"I like direct men."

"You mean, you like men you can direct."

"And the kind I can't direct?" She was smiling right into his eyes.

"I do believe you like me."

Her laughter tinkled over their glasses as both leaned their forearms on the table. He was aware that everyone in the room was watching, although no one was looking directly at them.

"I, for my part, like privacy," she said.

"Tell me what's on your mind. Or—on Ed Deal's mind."

He saw it go in. She hadn't been expecting that.

"So you think I'm working with Deal?"

He shook his head. "No. I know you are."

She dropped her eyes, looking down at her hand, which was lying on the table. Her fingers began to play lightly on the baize covering.

"All right, then," she said after a moment. "I do work with Ed. On certain things. He, after all, is the mayor—and the town's leading businessman. He's the only one in this place who gets anything done. And he needs someone like me. Someone who knows what's going on in the grapevine. You know that expression?"

"I have heard it a few hundred times. Yes, I know it."

"In that way I help him. We're old friends, Ed and I."

"So what do you want from me?"

She didn't answer right away, but he felt her knee brush his under the table. "You know what I want, Slocum."

"You mean, that's what Deal wants you to want, don't you?"

"I don't know what he wants. I only know what I want." And then she added, "I want this town to settle down. That's what Ed Deal wants—really. All this trouble and sweat over Cherokee Bill and that unfortunate boy, and now the disruption with the cattle herds and cowboys coming in. I've been in cow towns, Slocum. I know how rough it can be. Ed Deal has put a lot of time and money into Horse Creek, and naturally he wants to protect it. He wants to protect himself and he wants to protect the town. I don't see anything wrong in that. Do you?"

"No. Nothing wrong in that."

"Then . . . ?"

He stood up. "Then let's get down to some serious talk. In your private quarters."

"Jesus, Slocum, that's what I wanted to do in the first place, for chrissake!"

He had his hands on her even before she locked the door behind them, reaching around her from behind, feeling her pushing nipples, while he pressed his rigid organ in between her buttocks. Now, reaching down, he pulled up her dress and pulled down her underpants while she reached back and rubbed his erection. In the next moment he had his fly open and his cock in his hand, pushing it now between her cool white buttocks while she reached down to grab its head as it nestled into her bush from the rear. She was soaking wet.

Without a word, their breath panting, they dropped to the floor and he mounted her with her dress rolled up to her neck, his trousers halfway off, but with the thrust of his passion sliding deep into her while she moaned and gasped and began to walk across the floor on her hands and knees while he pumped her from the rear.

Frantically they tore at their clothes, trying not to miss a stroke. And finally they were naked, still moving over the floor as she held his balls, reaching back with one hand while he reached under her to hold her teats.

"Oh, God, Slocum—dear God, give, give, give it!" She stopped now and, laying her head down on her forearms, began to wiggle on the whole length of his huge organ.

"Lie on your back," she gasped.

In a moment he was down on his back and she was sitting on him, facing his feet, with her full, firm buttocks pumping up and down on his erection. He thought he would go out of his mind as she rode him.

Somehow he turned her over without removing himself, without losing their rhythm, and now he was on top, her legs spread wide to receive him, and he buried his face in her quivering, wet breasts, now taking one nipple in his mouth, now the other; riding her high and deep and now slowly, now quickly, now . . . to the ultimate climax as he squirted and squirted again and again and again into her, as she bit his shoulder to quiet the screams of ecstasy that wanted to break from her.

They lay together panting, his soft organ inside her still.

"My God," she said at last. "God, Slocum, where in the hell did you ever learn to fuck like that?"

"Right here," he said. "Right now."

She grinned in his ear as she felt his organ stirring inside her. "God almighty, you're not through?"

"Are you?"

She didn't answer, but her tongue started to lick his ear as his manhood grew again to fill her.

"God, it's like a fence post," she whispered as her buttocks began to move.

Slocum had her up on her shoulders, driving his cock even deeper into her, her legs wrapped around him as they bucked and wiggled and stroked until the last drop had come.

9

In the heated daze of the forenoon, the land appeared to shimmer, as though there were something uncertain in the air. And it was true that perception was tricky. At first the horse and its rider seemed indistinguishable from the stand of box elders through which they had appeared. But then, in movement, breaking away from the horizon, they became clear.

They moved slowly, the rider obviously looking carefully for sign, noting the eagle sweeping the top of sky and the jay that suddenly charged out of the willows near the creek. The rider seemed to become one with his horse as the animal's ears swept forward and up, questioning the intruder in the great silence that seemed to hold them, to bind them to the tawny land.

The man's entire body had keened to the warning. Shifting in his battered stock saddle, he eased the holstered six-gun at his right hip, brushing the hideout gun beneath his hickory shirt. Yet he maintained the slow, steady gait of the big blue roan.

In a matter of moments he was under cover again,

near willows and box elders, and he drew rein. Now he saw the coyote running low to the ground and he knew what had startled the jay. Still, he did not slacken his vigilance. He was a big man, broad with muscle and with bright blue eyes that here and there were almost merry as they picked carefully over his surroundings, going back again to the rim of the sky and returning to the foreground. He reached to his shirt pocket now and took out a cigar that had already been half smoked and lighted it, striking the wooden lucifer on his saddle horn. He put the match carefully back into his picket, blowing away the cloud of cigar smoke that appeared in the air around his head. Yes, he figured it was safe enough for a smoke. And his big hand touched the big skinning knife sheathed at his belt.

Seen close, he seemed a man in his middle years, with his eyes widely spaced and with crow's feet at their corners. Everything about him was big. He had a big nose. He crossed his forearms now and leaned forward onto the pommel of his creaking saddle and looked carefully through an opening in the trees at the dust cloud moving along the horizon on the other side of the creek.

For a good while he sat his roan horse watching the thick dust thrown by the herd of cattle as they moved east. He had been following the herd for some time, figuring out the time of their arrival at the new shipping pens in town.

He drew on his cigar. It was an old butt, but it tasted good even so. He would be glad when he could ride into town again and have some liquor, some women, some good smokes.

The rider looked up at the sun now, figuring the

time of day. It wouldn't be long. His eyes dropped
again to the cloud of dust that hid the cattle moving
toward the crossing at the Still Water River. Presently
he made out the horse and rider that detached themselves from the drag and rode in a fast canter toward
him.

"It faired off good," said the man called Hendry
Chimes.

Cherokee Bill Hagstrom shifted his weight a little
as the roan stuck out his right foreleg and bent to rub
his nose along it.

"Herd looks to be pretty good. Didn't run too
much off them on the drive."

Hendry Chimes spat over his horse's withers and
looked at the big man with the big nose. It was indeed difficult to tell what Cherokee's features were
under the thicket of wiry black hair. "Klanghorn's
good with the cattle. And he had the good sense to
let his trail boss run things." There was a tight,
mirthless grin on Hendry's face as he said this.

"You know this new marshal they got in town,
Hendry?"

"I met the son of a bitch. You know him?"

"Heard of him. Heard he rode with Quantrill. Not
when I was with Bloody Bill howsomever. Maybe he
could cause us a little trouble?"

Cherokee Bill was fishing and Chimes knew it,
but that was the way of it. A man had to find things
out in his own way. "You still figure it'll be best in
town?" Chimes asked.

"You got your men lined up?"

Hendry Chimes inclined his head.

Cherokee studied the hard, lined face and smiled

inside himself. He just hoped Chimes was nearly as good as his brother. Hendry—the older one—had been tough as a singletree and no man to look at cockeyed. Until he'd come up against John Slocum. Well, maybe he'd get a look-see at Slocum. He'd heard a lot about him, heard he'd rode with Quantrill. Of course, Chimes could double-deal him, though that wouldn't get him anywhere but fast dead. But he needed Chimes for his plan. And it was clear that Chimes needed him for his.

"When will you take over the herd?"

"At the stock pens."

"Klanghorn?"

"I'll likely have to kill him." Chimes spat again, swiftly this time, and the other man noted anger in it.

Cherokee sniffed. "You better start your stampede soon as you hit the first houses. I'll already be in town, watching for you. Thing is, to keep our lines clear. The town council—you don't know them, but they're my concern. I got a special plan for them. You'll take care of Klanghorn and any others then. Except—Slocum. I will take care of Slocum." He was looking hard at the trail boss whose brother had ridden with Bloody Bill Anderson and with Cherokee Bill Hagstrom.

Hendry Chimes was thinking how he needed Hagstrom, needed him to take care of the town. And he dropped his eyes, looking away.

Cherokee Bill grinned at that. But he wasn't fooled.

"The son of a bitch killed my brother," Chimes said.

"We'll see," Cherokee said. "Gimme some smokes."

"Remember, I will be taking the cattle," Chimes said. "'Course, there'll be our agreement on your slice."

"And I will take the town," Cherokee Bill said. And he grinned, revealing a few dark fangs through the hole that appeared in his beard. His blue eyes were twinkling. "And there'll be our agreement on *your* slice."

He was enjoying the cheroot that Hendry Chimes had brought him as he watched the trail boss ride back to the J. C. herd.

In the early evening, with the light still in the sky, even though the sun had gone behind the horizon, the three figures squatted around the sparse fire.

Felix was looking at the skinned knuckles on his left hand. "Son of a bitch had a head hard as a fucking billiard ball."

"You musta cracked him pretty hard," Lolly said admiringly. He ran the tip of his tongue along his cracked lips as he grinned at Felix.

Bile suddenly belched. "Shit, Lolly, if I hadn't've popped in there just then and helped old Felix here, he'd've bin in real trouble with that tough old coot!" And he started to roar with laughter at his joke.

The next thing he knew, he was flat on his face with his head almost in the fire and with Felix's knee right in the small of his back.

"You smart son of a bitch. Don't you never learn about trying to whipsaw old Felix! You dumb shit, you!"

"I was only jokin', fer chrissake...." Bile's words came gasping out of his pain. "Jesus, get me away from the fire!"

"Say please!"

"Fuck . . ."

"Not fuck. Please!"

Bile was struggling, but he could hardly move with Felix's knee in his back and the breath all but knocked out of him. But he finally managed to squeeze out the word. Both he and Lolly knew that Felix wouldn't have let him up without it. Indeed he would have stuck his head right into the fire.

As he sat now, trying to regain himself, Bile softened. The picture of the old man being knocked off his chair by Felix started a laugh in him. It came out of his throat in uneven spurts, for he was still regaining his breath. But the other two caught it, and now they were all three of them roaring with rich laughter.

"Bastard won't cross us again, will he, Felix?" Lolly said.

"Not this one," Felix snapped back, but he was still laughing at the picture of the old man pulling up his pants after he, Felix, had sliced his belt and galluses with his big skinning knife. "Lost his pants, he did." And this triggered another round of high laughter.

For several minutes now they retold the tale— how they had busted into the newspaper office and braced the old man for money and, when he'd told them to get out, had sliced him and beaten him.

"Tough old codger," Bile said.

"He ain't now," Felix said darkly. "He is lucky I didn't kill him when he tried to go for me, the bastard."

"He was lucky," repeated Lolly.

"But I wanted him to tell that Cherokee Bill had

visited him. Since he runs the newspaper. See, I figure we can run one more hit and then take off for
maybe—what? Where?"

"Californy," said Bile and Lolly in unison.

"Californy it is, by God!" said Felix. "But first
one more shot at the town. We don't want to run out
of money when we're out there, now do we?"

"Felix, you think it's safe? We might not be so
lucky trying again. People might be laying for us."

"It is safe. And it is what we be going to do."

Their voices floated into the night air. It was dark
now, and their faces glowed in the firelight. They
had been drinking, as usual. And it wasn't any time
at all before Bile and Lolly were right there with
Felix's feelings about how easy the pickings were
and that they could sure enough pull another shake-
down in the town. One more, just before the cattle
was due, was how Felix had put it. It made sense,
with everybody's attention on the expected arrival of
the Texas longhorns. Sure enough, they could do it.
Like rolling off a log, Felix had said.

They sat there a long time around the fire, drinking and talking and enjoying themselves. And finally
they grew tired and stretched out and slept. Their
snores rang into the night, disturbing no one. Least
of all the big man with the big nose and thick beard
who had been listening to them for a couple of hours.

Cherokee Bill was well hidden from them. He had
stumbled on their camp by chance and had remained
to listen to the tale of how they were milking the
townspeople of Horse Creek by using his name. He
had heard tidbits of gossip about what they were
doing, and he wasn't surprised. Hell, a man had to
make a living in this tough world any way he could

get away with. It occurred to him to kill them. He could have done that easily right now. But he decided not to. He had a better plan in mind. And he grinned into the soft night as he rode toward the town. He had a much better plan. One that also had its humor. Cherokee Bill was also famous for his sense of humor. And he was chuckling to himself now as he approached Horse Creek. In fact, he could hardly keep from breaking into loud laughter.

It was Kelly Kenton who had found Humboldt Smithers lying on the floor of his office. It was her habit to bring him supper and sometimes lunch, especially during the times when the work of the newspaper required long hours. This visit, however, was almost accidental. She was passing by on her way home late from the Wild Horse when she saw the light on and, on a sudden impulse, decided to stop in to see how his meal had been.

She found him lying on the floor, semiconscious; fortunately not very long after his attackers had left. His bleeding had stopped. He was badly shaken but nothing was broken, and a visit from the doctor revealed that Humbolt had no internal injuries.

"You're lucky, young man," the youthful doctor had said jovially in his best bedside manner.

"And you, sir, are lucky," rejoined the Colonel, "in being able to ply your profession under the practiced eye of one of medicine's elder statesmen. You did well. Not remarkably well. Just so. Be satisfied with small rewards. Nor will I offend you by offering you payment, except in kind. Call on me the next time you find yourself indisposed, Doctor."

Doctor Herbert Fillmore blushed all over his very

round head, averting his gaze from Kelly Kenton as, drenched in embarrassment, he took his departure.

"Good fellow," Humboldt exclaimed after he had gone. "He works hard. He is industrious. Alas, like so many in his profession, he lacks true intelligence. There is nothing *special* about him. Do you follow me?" He cocked his eye at the girl, his spirits fully returned, except for a slight, occasional shaking of his seventy-year-old hands.

"He is obviously not special the way you are, Colonel," Kelly said with a comfortable tone of voice and a warm, very fond smile.

"Or like Slocum," the Colonel said. "You know Slocum. He is special. Mark that. We are going to need him any moment now." And this time the Colonel detected the blush in Kelly's face.

The blush had only just faded when there came a knock at the door and in walked Slocum.

"Speak of the devil!" The Colonel's joyous laugh rose like a geyser in his throat and suddenly whipped him into a fit of uncontrollable coughing.

Slocum had heard the news of the Colonel's beating the moment he had returned to town and had come straight to the *Gazette*'s office. It was a great relief to see Humboldt in such good shape. And it was especially good to see Kelly.

"Who was it?" he asked. "Anything to do with Cherokee Bill?"

"The man said that's who he was. But I don't recollect Cherokee looking like that; except it was a helluva long time ago—excuse my language, please, young lady—and Cherokee seemed bigger. And he had that big nose. But—at my age, memory can do tricks on a man."

"He was alone?"

"You know, Slocum. He started to push me, and he went too far, and by golly, I popped him one. Knocked him right on his you-know-what. . . ." And he cut his eye fast to Kelly, blinking apologetically for speaking thus in front of a lady. "Only then his pals came in and they worked me over." He grinned painfully, and as he turned his head in the light Slocum saw the big bruise, the cuts around his eye. "Then . . . then I guess I lost consciousness. Conked out. But by the Lord Harry, give me back twenty years, and while I'd still be old enough to be that whippersnapper's father, I'd sure clean his clock! And I do not mean maybe!" In his excitement the old man charged to his feet but suddenly collapsed and fell back into the ancient chair, which under his falling weight went over backward with a crash.

"Lucky it was the leg of the chair that broke," Slocum said wryly as he and Kelly helped the Colonel to another seat. "Now, take it slow, will you!"

"What I need is a drink," Humboldt said. "Gimme. Gimme a drink—for the sake of—whatever . . ." He was rambling.

Slocum held him up while Kelly helped him swallow some whiskey. Then together they helped him to his cabin.

They sat with him a while and then Slocum walked the girl to her house. It was early evening now, and Slocum walked slowly. He was pleased to see that she was not in any hurry and kept to his slow, almost meandering pace.

"Have you been able to get deputies to help you?" Kelly asked.

"Not so's anybody'd notice," he answered with a

wry grin. And as he turned halfway to face her as they walked, his hand brushed hers accidentally. He felt the thrill run through him. And he thought he saw her eyes glisten.

"I am taking you to supper after the herd gets in," he said. "That is, as soon as things get a bit settled."

"Are you telling me or asking?" Her tone was amused.

"I am telling you."

"I see."

They had reached her house.

"Dad said he thought you'd been having trouble getting men to be deputies."

"That is so. But sometimes it's better to work alone."

"I'd make a pretty good deputy, I think."

"I might take you up on that."

"And Dad said he could too."

"I know."

He could still see her face in the fading light; really, he could feel her face more than see it. Suddenly she took a step forward and kissed him on the cheek.

"I accept your—uh—invitation to supper."

And she was gone, the door closing quietly behind her.

As Slocum walked down the street every nerve in his body was tingling, and his erection was giving him trouble in walking. It was a while before it subsided and he felt normal again. He told himself that the next time—next time he was going to have her or he would simply explode. And he knew, too, that he hadn't felt such a powerful desire in a good while. There was just something very special about Kelly

Kenton. And for a moment in his mind he went over her imagined assets—breasts, buttocks, thighs, and that marvelous hairy orifice between her legs. All that—yes. But something more. Her totality exceeded by far any kind of addition of her parts.

In the twilight the lamps of the town glowed in a special way, neither wholly in the day nor the nighttime but in both.

Slocum had almost reached the marshal's office when he heard, then almost immediately saw, the two riders as they came from the far end of town. The Texas yell cut into the street like a skinning knife slicing right to the bone, while they bore down, lifting a great cloud of dust.

He felt something tighten inside him, then let go —something very familiar, it was—as he raised the sawed-off shotgun and walked out into the middle of the street. There weren't many people about, and those few that had been out had quickly moved inside at the sound of those Texas yells.

The Greener 12-gauge was pointed right at the two cowboys as they drew rein fast in front of him, in a wall of dust.

They were young, bearded, covered with the dust of the trail, and their horses were lathered. There was no stopping them with any kind of look, or maybe even with the presence of that wicked cut-down Greener. Slocum knew from past, bitter experience that at such a moment there was really only himself.

"Well, lookee here! Man's got a shotgun, by God!"

Slocum felt the absolute emptiness of the street around him. "There is no racing horses in this town," he said. "Go back and read that sign down there where you came in off the trail. And no guns, neither. You can check them in any saloon or the marshal's office."

His words came out clean and even as a newly dealt hand. And then, "Other than that, boys, welcome to Horse Creek."

The one nearest him was grinning, his face wet with excitement. "And who are you, mister? Who the hell are you?"

"I am the marshal of this town."

"Where is your tin badge—huh!" He turned to his companion, the laughter roaring out of him.

"My badge? It is right here, boys." And the click of the shotgun hammer drawn back was as loud as a pistol shot in the empty street.

"I do mean right now," Slocum said.

"Sure, Marshal," the second young cowboy said. "Sure." Both of them were suddenly sober as a dry wood fence. "Where is the place to check our guns?"

"Yonder." He pointed the shotgun in the direction of the Last Drop, which was the nearest saloon. "But ain't you boys from the J. C.?"

"That's right, Marshal."

"What you doing in town, then? You're not due here till tomorrow."

"Just slipped away to check the way of life here, Marshal. Didn't mean no harm."

"Klanghorn send you in?" But he knew the answer to that.

"Nope."

"You tell Hendry Chimes the town is still here. And we will be expectin' you tomorrow. You got that straight?"

The two heads nodded, and without a word they turned their feisty horses.

"And walk them animals out of town."

Which they did, Slocum's eyes following them all the way down the street until they hit the trail back to the J. C. herd.

The sky was still holding some daylight as he finished his rounds. Then he went down to the Hello Eats for his supper, just in case any smart aleck had been taking note of his habit of going to the Wild Horse. No point asking for trouble when he was going to get all there was without asking for it.

10

There was no moon, and as Slocum stepped into the
Street he had to adjust to the dark quickly. Many of
the townsfolk had gone home and locked their doors
after hearing those two cowboys riding fast in and
out of town and firing their pistols in the air. For this
was the night before the first cattle drive was expected. Everyone knew about cow towns, even those
who had never been in Abilene, Dodge, or Ellsworth. The street was no place to be when those
cowboys, hot off the trail, hit town. And so this night
in the houses the curtains were drawn and lights were
either extinguished or their wicks were lowered. A
window light was a fine target for a sauced-up cow
waddy.

Slocum had made strong efforts to get a couple of
deputies, at the least, but to little avail. The turn-
downs had been numerous, the excuses always rea-
sonable. Only one had agreed, and Slocum had
demurred, for Idle Jeff Gowanus, though willing,
was not always reliable. Nobody could figure
whether he was "touched" or just indolent. Idle was a

sometime swamper in the Last Drop; a lanky young
lad with a loose jaw. He reminded people of Dummy
Jensen, except that he could speak and he wasn't
deaf. But he was slow.

"Jesus," Colonel Humboldt Smithers had said
when Slocum informed him who his one and only
deputy was, "that young feller is slow as ice melting
in January."

"He's got two hands," Slocum said. "And he can
pack a gun."

"You will need more than one tin star to pin him
together," was Humboldt's tart rejoinder. "I figure
you would do better with yours truly."

"No. I don't want somebody age seventy—if you
ain't lying, which I believe you are—who has just
been beat up, looking like he was run over two, three
times by a hay wagon and a team of horses. Hell,
when we get this town cleaned up, somebody might
want to take our pictures. Never know!"

That had settled that. So he had Idle with him,
across the street at the present moment, checking
doors and windows, rooflines, and especially alleys.
For though the drive wasn't expected till the following forenoon, there was the good chance that some of
the drovers might be feeling previous. Like the pair
who had already ridden in. And Slocum knew that it
had to be upon the first batch of raunchy, thirsty
cowpokes that the impression had to be made.

And his expectations bore fruit. There were four
of those feisty drovers calling at the Three Aces.
Slocum wondered whether they had slipped away
from the vigilance of Hendry Chimes or had maybe
been sent in for some purpose. If so, he could only
wonder what.

But if Chimes was anything at all like his brother, the original Hendry, it could only mean trouble. Hendry Chimes. Some said he'd been Bloody Bill Anderson's right hand. The brother. Older for sure than the present Hendry, who, for some strange reason, had taken his brother's name. Hero worship very likely, Slocum reasoned. Some hero. Bloody Bill, a bare second to Quantrill in wanton cruelty; and Hendry Chimes, close enough to Bloody Bill to be his shadow. But like so many crazy gun-swifts, he couldn't stand anyone being better. Slocum had decided Hendry was going to have to stand it—lying down.

Slocum knew he was no one to point a finger over violence. He'd been through the worst of the war. Riding with Quantrill, to be sure, had been under Army orders. That didn't mean he'd liked it. Chimes, and others of his stripe, had clearly liked it. He'd seen that right off. And when Slocum had seen him setting fire to a sorrel pony who'd thrown him, he'd called him, and Chimes hit leather. Since his brother had taken his name, then he couldn't be all that much different. Slocum was certain of that.

As they came level with the Three Aces, Slocum told his deputy to stay across the street and cover the door of the saloon. For a moment he studied the four still-heated cow ponies at the hitch rail outside the saloon. It was dark in the street except for the lights coming from the Three Aces, the Last Drop, the Silver Dollar, the Double Dice, and the Buffalo Bar. Other than these places of pleasure, liquid and otherwise, the town of Horse Creek was still.

Slocum listened for a moment to the tinkle of the piano, the laughter, and now and then a random gunshot. And it dawned on him that the visit might well be deliberate, ordered by Klanghorn or Chimes. It had to be Chimes. Why would Klanghorn want to make trouble? Unless...unless what? He had learned from Godiva in a weak moment when her guard had been down, that Ed Deal and a couple of the council had ridden out to the J. C. herd and talked with Klanghorn.

Only there was no time now for thought.

More gunshots cut through the saloon, and the laughter grew even louder. He knew there had to be at least some twenty people inside, and somebody was bound to catch lead if he confronted them on the premises. But there was no other way. He had to establish the law right now—not later, when the boys were too drunk to realize what was happening. He wondered if Godiva was in her back room. And that gave him an idea.

In a moment he had walked through the alley to the back of the building. There was a light showing at a chink in the drawn curtain that covered her windows. He wondered if she had company. But he didn't wonder for long. There was no time to waste now. He tapped on the window and checked to see if he could open it. It was locked, but in a moment the curtain was parted just enough for someone to look out. He took a chance that it was her.

A moment later the window was raised. He got a whiff of her cigar.

"Slocum! Why didn't you come in the front? Afraid of all the big noise, or were you really spying on me?"

He saw she was half teasing him, half giving him a dig for not calling on her sooner.

"Let me in." He was already climbing over the sill, and now she drew the curtain all the way back to let him enter.

"You surprise me!"

"I wasn't aiming to surprise you. I want to get into the saloon without coming through the front."

"You mean, you're playing marshal and not lover. Shit!" She was really crestfallen, he could see. But he realized for the first time that she did have a sense of humor.

"I'll explain it later," he said, giving her a pat on her rump. "Business first."

"You've got a helluva nerve busting in here like this."

"I've got a helluva nerve humping the mayor's girlfriend, don't you think?"

"I see you get around. You know that Humboldt Smithers has one helluva big mouth."

"I know. I know. And you've got a couple of helluva big teats. Now step aside. I'll see you later and we'll have a little chat."

"Suppose I call some help. I've got men out there. You can't handle them all, Slocum."

"Do you want me to come back here and handle you?" he said, covering his annoyance at her interrupting his action.

"Yes. Yes, I do. And soon. I've missed you, you big bastard." And she stared down at his crotch.

"I'll be back," he said, and stepped to the door.

"One of my men is right outside," she said, moving quickly toward him and touching his arm. "You'd better let me."

It was Oren guarding the door, and his eyebrows shot up when he saw Slocum; but he said nothing.

The attention of everyone in the room at that moment was on a group around the upright piano. The piano player, a tiny man named Piece Minor, sat quivering in his chair with the tallest man Slocum had ever seen standing over him. He was well over six feet.

"Let's see if you can dance, Shorty! On account of you sure as hell can't play that pianner!" The tall Texan roared the words into the room and now drew his six-gun and fired at the piano player's feet.

"Dance, by God! Get off yer ass and dance!"

In a moment the tall Texan's three companions had joined the fun and were firing at the little man's feet while he hopped and jumped and skipped and just barely kept from falling.

Slocum stood next to Oren just outside Godiva's door, aware that she was watching the scene from behind him. A couple of the clientele had seen him by now, and he signaled them not to draw attention to his presence. The Texans, anyway, were too engrossed in their frolic to realize the law had entered the scene. Slocum waited.

Suddenly the firing stopped. "Hell, I got to reload!" the tall Texan shouted.

From out in the street came the muffled sound of three gunshots.

"Save it," Slocum said then, stepping forward, with the Greener sawed-off shotgun pointed right at the group of cowboys. "I will take those guns. Just hand them to Mr. Minor there. Piece, you take 'em."

Piece Minor was shaking all over. His face was sheer white; there was sweat on his cheeks.

"Give him a drink," Slocum said to the bartender.

It was what was needed. Piece managed to pull

himself together then, and collected the Texans' artillery.

"Marshal, we were just having a little entertainment," said one of the Texans, and Slocum saw he was one of the pair he'd already ordered out of town.

"You are going to have your entertainment without either guns or horses if you run those animals in the street or shoot off your pop pistols."

"Marshal," said one of the cowboys with a boozy laugh. "You don't know who you are talking to. You are talking to Texans!" And he almost doubled over with laughter, while his companions joined in.

"And you, mister, are talking to me!"

But there was something he didn't like. He could feel it in his guts. Of old, he'd known that sign so well. But what? He had them covered with the shotgun. Slocum couldn't figure why he felt so uneasy, yet it was there. Only there was nothing to do but just what he was doing.

"This here's a warning," he said. "Next time yer asses get thrown in jail. Now git on and git out!"

It was just as he said those words that he remembered the three gunshots he'd heard out in the street.

He had turned slightly to take in a better view of the side of the room. He would always remember that moment. He would always remember Idle Jeff Gowanus.

As his eyes came in line with the bar mirror, he saw the two men almost directly behind him, heard the click of metal. In that instant he dropped and spun, bringing round the sawed-off Greener scattergun before he hit the floor on his back.

Later Oren put it that they'd had to pick up the

pair of bushwackers with a couple of wet cloths—
what was left of them.

But it was Slocum who picked up Idle Jeff—the
man who everyone said didn't have the sense of a
jackass, the only man who'd stood by him as deputy
—and buried him, bullet holes and all.

Slocum told it to Humboldt Smithers that same
night. "I want you to write about Idle in your paper.
Somebody—maybe Chimes, maybe Cherokee Bill
Hagstrom, maybe J. C. Klanghorn or Ed Deal—set
me up," he said. "I heard those shots that killed Idle.
Those shots that killed Idle Jeff saved my life."

It had been close. One of the bushwackers' bullets
had grazed him, giving him a stiff right arm. Not
good. The question was who had set him up like that.
The Texans had been in on it, he was sure; maybe
unwittingly, but still, they had an air about them afterward, as though they knew something. He'd ordered them all out of town. And now he was
wondering if it had been Chimes. Or maybe Cherokee Bill had gotten his nose in the wind and was
trying to head him off before an inevitable show-
down. Did the big man know he was on his trail?

There was something else bothering him, nagging
at the edge of his thoughts. It had been there awhile,
but nothing had formed; no hard thought with which
he could proceed.

He had felt this unspoken question especially
while talking with Kelly Kenton and her father in the
early morning after the shooting in the Three Aces.

They had been sitting in the Kenton kitchen in the
log cabin Tom Kenton had built on the outskirts of

town. When Slocum had taken time to admire the construction, it had opened up the older man.

"I'm just noticing how tight those joints are," Slocum had said, feeling along one of the logs to the corner of the room where the log's notch made the right angle where the companion wall met it.

"Didn't have any tool but a ax," Kenton said proudly with a shy grin.

"No adz, no saw?" Slocum asked in surprise.

"Not a single nail."

"It is sure solid."

"Tight and warm and snug," Kelly said, coming in just then from the kitchen. "This was the main room. I remember when that was all we had, just the one. My mom used to cook on that jumbo stove there before we got the range."

Slocum grinned at her. "That how come you're such a good cook?" he said.

"It's all spruce," Tom Kenton said, coming in again to one of his favorite subjects. "Felled 'em up on the north fork, snaked 'em down with a old crow bait I had for a workhorse—peeled with a ax."

"No drawknife?"

"Just the ax—for everything. Took a while longer, but I didn't have no tools then. The ax was borrowed from Miles Miller, and when I gave it back to him, it was just as sharp and clean as when I'd borrowed it."

The three had a chuckle at that, and Slocum lifted his mug of coffee. "I hate to ask you some questions, but I've got to."

"You're the marshal, ain'tcha?" Kenton's voice was a little tight but not unfriendly.

"I was thinking about Dummy Jensen. Kelly, you say Norah used to teach him, give him lessons."

"Well, in a way. You know he was deaf and dumb. Not so easy to communicate when a party is that way."

"She had him drawing stuff, I believe," Kenton said. "I recollect a box of colored pencils."

"And they knew the sign language, what the Indians use. The Shoshone—and others, too, I guess," Kelly said.

"But could he read or write?"

"I don't know how he could have," Kelly said, "since he was born without hearing and not able to speak. I'm pretty sure Norah couldn't have taught him. I mean, how would you even begin with somebody like that."

"That's just what I was thinking," Slocum said.

They sat for a moment in silence while Slocum finished his coffee. Then Tom Kenton got up and said he'd better be getting to his work. There'd likely be horses to shoe when the drovers got to town.

"What can I do to help?" Kelly asked Slocum when they were at the door of the cabin.

"You can have supper with me when this thing gets a little settled."

He heard her breath catch, saw the flickering in her eyes.

"I'll have supper with you anytime you want, Mr. Slocum."

His heart was singing as he walked down the street. He had decided to call on some members of the town council.

*   *   *

The herd would be due within sir or seven hours, he was thinking as he stepped into the Ajax Feed and Hardware and was met by Parker Tilbury. He was still wondering why Klanghorn had been holding the herd at Crazy Woman Creek. He was pretty sure now that it was connected with the Texans in the Three Aces. And he knew that by the time those cowboys hit town, they would be on fire for action. Well, he had his Greener and his Colt. Mostly he had himself.

"What kin I do for you, Marshal?" Tilbury's voice was big, expansive, eager with the excitement of the approaching day. It was quiet now, but the storm would come. And, in fact, Slocum had noted the clouds gathering along the horizon and the wet smell in the early-morning air. Yes, the storm could be of two kinds.

"Wanted to talk to you a minute, Tilbury."

"Sure enough. We can set." And the storekeeper moved over to some chairs that were standing around the potbellied stove, which was cold now, but even so, still served as the center of social life in the store.

When he was seated, Slocum looked over at Tilbury, measuring him. And he wanted the man to know he was doing just that: checking on his honesty.

"Yes, sir," said Parker Tilbury, beginning to feel nervous.

"I heard there was a letter found in Dummy Jensen's pocket either at the time he was hanged or pretty soon after. Can you tell me anything about that?"

Tilbury's lips began to work, he blinked rapidly, sniffed, and even started to reach to his crotch to scratch or maybe just to support himself but refrained at the last instant.

"Marshal, I don't know anything about a letter and Dummy Jensen. See, I wasn't at that hanging, and I don't know anything about it. Seems to me— well, you'd have to get hold of somebody who was there."

"Who was there?"

Tilbury's shrug was almost violent. "Search me. I got no idea."

"And you never heard about a letter to Dummy Jensen from his brother Cherokee Bill."

"No, sir. No, sir, I have not. I have heard that Cherokee is supposed to be that boy's brother, and there are rumors in town that Cherokee will be coming in for a visit. But I know nothing about it. I got nothing to fear on that. I wasn't anywhere near any of it!"

The obvious person to ask in the first place, Slocum well knew, would have been the undertaker, Ed Deal. But he had his plan, which was to shake up the council, see if anyone might make a slip.

But Tod Ollenburgh and Clem Dunstan gave him the same response as Tilbury. Neither of them knew anything. Neither had been at the lynching, though Dunstan said he had been in one of the posses that had ridden out to look for the killer; only he hadn't gone any farther than that. John Bettman had a touch of the croup and his wife said he couldn't talk to anybody, but he'd be up and about later that morning. That left the mayor-banker-undertaker. That left Ed Deal.

The bank wasn't open yet, but he could see somebody moving around inside, and when he knocked on the door, it was Deal who opened it.

"Ah, good morning, Slocum. Ready for the high action today, are we?" He stepped back to allow Slocum to step inside the bank, then closed the door firmly behind him.

"Come on in," Deal continued. "I've got some coffee here on my stove. Good thing to have in a bank, don't you think, a stove." And he chuckled. He was in his shirt sleeves, with garters around his arms, which made Slocum wonder whether the head of the bank also performed a teller's tasks. But he didn't hold the thought as he followed Deal into another room.

"What can I do for you, Marshal?" Deal asked, handing him a mug of coffee which he'd filled from the pot on the little corner stove in his office.

It was just as he was accepting the coffee that Slocum smelled the musk. He turned to the other door of the room just as Deal offered him a cigar.

"I've already had some early-morning visitors," Deal said easily, having caught what Slocum had noticed. "Depositors do worry sometimes, though they've no need to."

"I wanted to ask you—in your role as undertaker —if you could tell me what you found in Dummy Jensen's pockets when his body was brought in."

"Not much, I'm afraid. The boy wasn't rich by any means. Some change, and I believe a top. It would be in the drawer of my desk at my other office, the mortuary office."

"No letter. Nothing like that?"

"A letter? What would that boy be doing with a letter?"

"I'd heard stories," Slocum said easily. "That there was a letter from his brother."

"You mean, Cherokee?"

"Cherokee Bill Hagstrom."

Deal nodded thoughtfully as he sipped his coffee. "Well, to be sure, there is that story that a letter was found on the body from Cherokee, who turned out to be Dummy's brother. We all know it—but as rumor. After all, if anyone would have seen a letter, it would have been myself—unless, of course, somebody, one of the party who hanged that unfortunate boy, had removed it. But as the Horse Creek undertaker, I went through the body's pockets—as part of my duties before burial—and found nothing that even resembled a letter. Though, of course, I—like everybody else—have heard about it." He opened his hands wide, offering the question. "What more can I say? Eh?"

"Just thought I'd like to take a look at it," Slocum said.

"You're questioning then whether a deaf and dumb person such as Jensen could read? Is that it? I see no reason why not. But actually, I hadn't even thought about it."

Slocum saw he was getting nowhere, although he had expected to gain some ground. His purpose had been to shake the council members. And while nothing obvious had appeared to implicate any one of them, he could see that they were shaken. Except perhaps for Deal.

It was about the middle of the forenoon when he got to the marshal's office and sat down at his desk. He'd been there just a few minutes when Colonel Humboldt Smithers walked in.

"Any time now," Slocum said as the Colonel took a chair. "How are you feeling, Colonel?"

"Fit!" He grinned slyly. "I followed your orders to the decimal point! I believe I make an excellent deputy!"

"What happened?"

"I stationed myself in the Double Dice, close to the bank, as you suggested."

"And . . ."

"And I saw not one, not two, but four members of Horse Creek's town council hurrying to the bank before it was open for business. In other words . . ." He let it hang.

"They were calling on Mr. Deal."

"I had drawn exactly the same conclusion, Marshal Slocum!" The Colonel's portentous tone was accompanied by his sly grin and a wink.

"Good enough."

"Are you thinking what I am thinking?" the Colonel asked.

"That there was no letter in Dummy's pocket but that Deal said there was?"

"Precisely!"

"And that Deal is double-crossing his fellow council members."

"On the target, Slocum!" The Colonel clapped his hands with pleasure.

"And . . ."

"And that Cherokee Bill Hagstrom maybe never wrote a letter to his brother at all!" The Colonel was fidgeting in his chair with excitement. "What a deal. Deal has dealt a deal is what I am saying!" And he broke into a high laugh. "That Ed Deal, for all he looks like a professional mourner, could slicker the drawers off a nun without laying a finger on her!"

Slocum was silent.

"You are thoughtful, Slocum. I think you are not wholly satisfied with our deductions."

Slocum reached to his shirt pocket and took out a quirly and lighted it. "I am not," he said.

"You see a hole in the argument somewhere. A loophole. That it?"

Slocum had been tilting back in his chair, and now he let the legs drop down and leaned forward on his desk. His forehead wrinkled; he was still wearing his Stetson hat, and the wrinkles moved up toward his hairline as he squinted at Humboldt Smithers. At that moment there was a splatter of raindrops against the windowpane.

"Thought so," muttered the Colonel. "Saw it was fixing to storm some. Not going to help the cattle any coming in with mud."

But Slocum wasn't concerned, and the Colonel returned to their conversation. "What have you got, Slocum?"

Slocum took the quirly out of his mouth. He looked down at his hands as he leaned even more heavily on his desk.

"What would you say if I told you Cherokee Bill Hagstrom doesn't have a brother . . ."

The Colonel's mouth dropped open. "What— what do you mean?"

"Figure it out, Colonel."

"You know that Cherokee doesn't have a brother? Is that it? That somebody—likely Deal—has been pulling a sandy on the boys?"

"That's the size of it, Humboldt."

"Deal figures to take over the town for himself, and he used the lynching as a lever."

Slocum nodded.

"And the fear of Cherokee coming in."

"He can knock off his council when he's good and ready, and it will be blamed on Hagstrom."

"That son of a bitch." Humboldt shook his head in awe. "But how did you know about Cherokee? How do you know he doesn't have a brother?"

"I don't know, Colonel. I am guessing."

"Glory be to God!" The Colonel's eyes were popping right out of his head. "No letter and no brother. Why, that Deal is some dealer, let me say it!"

"Thing is, it doesn't help me get any closer to finding Cherokee Bill Hagstrom," Slocum said. "Looks like I've been up a polecat's trail. And I'll have to start over."

"You're still marshal of Horse Creek, howsomever," said the Colonel. "And we need your protection against the likes of Ed Deal, not to mention those crazy Texas cowboys when they hit town."

Slocum was checking his Colt, the Greener shotgun, and finally the Winchester, which was lying across an empty nail keg.

"I am at your service, Marshal Slocum. Give me a gun."

"Take that Winchester there. You know how to handle 'er?"

"Don't be ridiculous! I was handling weaponry when you were still knee-high to a tumbleweed, sir!"

It was still early morning when the three wolfers walked into the Three Aces and ordered beer. Save for Oren the big bartender and a lone customer at a table in the far corner, the saloon was deserted.

The customer who sat by himself had been there since before dawn. He sat quietly, nursing beer, and appeared to be deep in thought. Oren had thought he was vaguely familiar, but then he let it go. There were an awful lot of men drifting through Horse Creek, especially during the past six months.

When the wolfers came in, he recognized them instantly. It didn't make him happy having Cherokee Bill Hagstrom and his two companions moving into the Three Aces, and he was about to see if he could whistle up some help in case of trouble when the big man with the whiskers called him over to the corner table.

"When does the bank open?" the big man asked.

"Should be any minute now," said Oren, glad to be away from the eyes of the three men across the room. "He usually opens on time."

The big man leaned forward. "Know the name of them fellers over to that table, do you?"

Oren didn't want to say anything, but he didn't like the look in the big man's eyes, so he decided to go with it.

"One of them is Cherokee Bill Hagstrom, and I guess the other two are just with him. I dunno."

"I see. And who is it runs the bank?"

"Why, Ed Deal. You'll meet him. He is the mayor of this town. A good man."

Cherokee Bill Hagstrom, to whom the bartender was talking—though he had no way of knowing it—nodded. His eyes returned to the wolfers. He had heard plenty when he'd listened to them at their camp fire a night ago. All that he needed to know for his plan to take form. And again—as he had done that night riding away from their camp—he chuckled deeply at the prospect of what lay in store for the three wolfers and especially the big one, the one named Felix, the one who'd been calling himself Cherokee Bill.

He stood up and walked out of the saloon, the three men at the other table hardly noticing him. In just a few minutes he was at the bank, which Ed Deal was just opening. As the banker pushed back the front door and saw his first customer, Cherokee Bill spoke.

"You be the bank manager, sir?"

"Yes sir, I'm Ed Deal."

"I wonder if you can help me. My name is Bill Hagstrom, and I'm just in town now to see what I can find out about my brother, Olaf Jensen. I figure a bank man might know this kind of thing better than anybody."

Cherokee Bill watched the bank manager and mayor of Horse Creek change color.

"I don't know much about it, but I could find out. As you say, a banker has connections, and certainly a mayor does," he added with a little laugh.

"I heerd that Olaf died under bad circumstances, and I want to get that cleared up."

"I understand, sir. I wonder if you would come back, say tomorrow. I could have news for you then."

"See you tomorrer."

Cherokee turned on his heel and left, but he didn't go far. He walked far enough to be out of sight, but then cut back quickly behind some buildings and reappeared in the alley beside the bank. He was waiting there, out of sight, when Ed Deal came out into the street.

It was easy enough to follow him to the four houses of the four members of the council. He had heard their names from the wolfers out on the prairie, but this method saved time, and it also amused Cherokee's sense of humor. All he had to do now was wait.

Within an hour the town council met with Ed Deal in the back room of the Last Drop. Cherokee had watched them go in, mentally checking their names against the names and descriptions he'd overheard from the wolfers. Satisfied that they were all in one place at last, he grinned and walked into the Last Drop, ordered a beer, and waited near the door of the back room.

Cherokee was wearing a big coat, which looked almost like a tent on him, for he himself was huge. Still, the coat was a good deal bigger than it seemed necessary, for it had to accommodate a number of weapons he kept about his person, a habit he'd acquired while riding with Bloody Bill Anderson. Weapons, he well knew, were always handy in his line of work.

And indeed the two six-guns proved mighty handy as the members of the council broke up their meeting and came out the door.

There weren't enough customers in the Last Drop that early in the morning for Cherokee to worry about anything like a flanking attack, and so he just blasted away, killing Parker Tilbury, John Bettman, Clem Dunstan, and Tod Ollenburgh. Ed Deal, the one he'd figured for the head of it, had not come out of the room. When Cherokee burst into the back room, he saw the open window. The banker had flown.

No matter, he told himself. He'd made his point, at least the first part—that this damn town better not go around using his name in vain. Now he grinned, thinking of the second part of his plan as he headed for the Three Aces.

The wolfers were still at their table. It was only a little before ten o'clock as Cherokee sidled up to them.

"What you want, mister?" Felix laid his palm flat down on the table and glared at the big man who had approached out of the semidarkness.

"You Cherokee Bill—huh?"

"Who says so?" Felix's hand moved toward his gun.

"I got to talk to you, Cherokee. Private. It can't wait."

Felix looked into those unflinching eyes and made his decision. "Drift," he said to his companions, "But not too far."

"Ed Deal, the mayor, is setting you up for a lynching," Cherokee said.

"What the hell! You funnin' me, for chrissake? What the hell you think yer doin'!"

"All you got to do is walk over to the Last Drop and see what he done to Tilbury and them others on the town council. I'm talking about the men who lynched your brother. You'll be called on those killings. I know the marshal is one tough son of a bitch."

For a moment Felix stared at the real Bill Hagstrom. "Obliged, stranger," he said. He stood up and signaled his two companions, who followed him out of the saloon.

The real Cherokee Bill Hagstrom poured himself a drink from the bottle the wolfers had left. He took his time drinking it. Some customers came into the saloon. The town was getting into action. Word came that the cattle would reach town later than expected.

Cherokee walked to the bar. He turned and faced the room. "Cherokee Bill Hagstrom," he shouted at the top of his lungs, "has just murdered the men who lynched his brother!"

Then he bought himself a drink. He figured it wouldn't take much longer than a half hour for the mob to catch up with Felix and his two pals.

That left the cattle herd, but Chimes could have it. And he could have Slocum too. Slocum meant nothing to him. And when someone came in and told that the three wolfers had been shot down trying to get out of town, a shout went up from the crowd that had gathered. Cherokee Bill was dead! And the man at the bar ordered another drink and grinned happily. Maybe this was the best one he'd ever pulled—ever!

11

Meanwhile Horse Creek lay in the somnolence of high noon. Yet within that near lethargy there was the burr of excitement; both regarding the approaching herd of cattle due at the loading pens any hour now and the ending of Cherokee Bill Hagstrom and the two members of his gang. The wipeout of four members of the town council balanced the excitement. None of those four had been overly popular, yet they had done their job more or less; and it was a blow to the town itself to lose four of its officers just like that. But Cherokee Bill had exacted the supreme penalty. They had indeed lynched the wrong man. No one believed Dummy Jensen was the guilty party in the murder and rape of which he'd been accused. The four councilmen had paid the price for their impetuosity, and Cherokee had paid for his. It was a clean slate. All were grateful that the mayor had been spared.

Slocum wondered otherwise. He wondered why Deal hadn't been killed. When he'd questioned the banker, Deal told him of his escape through the back window.

"I was damn lucky, that's all," he said.

And for the present Slocum was satisfied. Yet there were other aspects of the affair that puzzled him. First of all, he was pretty sure that the Cherokee Bill who had been killed along with his two companions was indeed a fake. The real Cherokee—from what he knew of him—would never have fallen into such a trap. All along he had felt that the wolfers were simply riding in on the real Cherokee's coattails. But, of course, where was the question of proof. As far as citizen opinion went, Cherokee Bill was dead; and as for the law, what could anyone "prove"? Cherokee Bill, for all intents and purposes, was "dead," thus he was free.

His arm was sore, and it was his gun arm. The bullet in the Three Aces had come close to being bad trouble, and at any other time he simply would have waited until the soreness wore off. But now he needed his arm.

He had been having coffee in Denver House, and when he went out into the street, he felt the thunder in the air again, even though the sky was clear. The gathering was felt all over town. People looked at the sky, reading for sign, even though nothing could be seen. When Slocum started down the street toward the marshal's office, he had wiped all thoughts out of his mind. There was nothing now but the business at hand. The Klanghorn herd and Hendry Chimes. For he was sure the men in the Three Aces who had tried to kill him had been sent by Chimes.

Just as he reached the door of his office he heard it. At first it was like a distant buzzing or rumbling.

It grew louder until somebody far down the street yelled, "It's the cattle! The cattle are coming!" And the shout was taken up now as men appeared in the street to bring their children and women into their homes.

Slocum was already running down the dirt street telling everyone to get inside. In moments the street was deserted, except for the approaching yelling of the oncoming drovers and the bawling and drumming of the J. C. herd.

Slocum stood still in the middle of the empty street, listening. The cattle were not running, but the sound of their hooves could be heard above anything else. Then he realized that a drop of water had struck the back of his hand, and he saw that he'd forgotten the weather in the urgency of the moment. At the same instant the sky darkened as though something had been pulled over it, and the sun was completely gone.

In the next moment lightning forked the stygian sky, and a crack of thunder shook the town. Looking south, Slocum saw the leaders of the herd breaking wild-eyed down the street. The leaders were jogging now, still clearing the wooden walks and pillars that supported the canopies. But those crowding behind were not so nimble, and here and there a post was struck.

Suddenly shots rang out, fired from the rear of the herd. Slocum swore as some animals hit one of the canopy posts and knocked it down, and the porch it had been supporting tumbled into the mass of charging, panicking beef. Quickly he mounted his spotted pony, which had been hitched outside the Double Dice.

"It's a stampede!" somebody shouted as more shots were fired.

Slocum rode quickly toward the charging cattle, using his lariat rope, which he'd folded over as a whip to beat the leaders on their snouts to try to turn them. He saw J. C. Klanghorn breaking through an alley to try to head off the longhorns with a quirt.

"Who the hell fired those goddamn guns!" Slocum shouted to the cattleman.

"He's gonna be damn sorry and damn dead when I catch him!" Klanghorn shouted back.

But between them they could do nothing with the roaring herd. The beasts were out of control. Lightning again slashed the town, and thunder shot across the sky as the herd of cattle became a torrent of beef. Rain was beating down into the dust that was filling the air and which would soon be mud.

"We can't stop 'em." Slocum shouted to Klanghorn. "I'm cutting back to see who's firing those shots!"

He spurred his horse into an alley, then galloped up the back street to the rear of the herd. He could hear porches crashing to the street as their posts were knocked down, the cries of the cowboys, the bellowing of the beeves, and more shots.

When he came through another alley behind the drive, he saw a surging sea of cattle wiping down through the middle of the town, destroying anything that got in its way. Slocum had been in stampedes before but never anything like this.

The cowboys had scattered out to the sides, riding into other alleys and even through house yards to give the crazed animals free movement.

Suddenly he saw Hendry Chimes standing on

what remained of the Ajax Feed and Hardware porch.

"Slocum!"

The spotted pony screamed as Chimes's bullet hit it, and it staggered and went to its knees. Chimes's second bullet knocked the hat off Slocum's head as he landed in the dust of the street, which was rapidly turning to mud.

"I'm killing you, you son of a bitch, Slocum!"

Slocum had landed on his sore arm, his gun arm, and there was no chance to draw. There was nothing else to do but roll in the hope of getting under a nearby porch.

He heard Klanghorn's voice calling Chimes and cursing. And then two shots, and as he reached the porch he saw the cattleman tumble out of his saddle.

Chimes had lost his hat and was standing wild-eyed in the debris of the smashed porch of the feed store. His gun was pointing directly at Slocum after he had shot Klanghorn.

"I am going to kill you, Slocum. I've got you dead, you son of a bitch!"

Slocum was half on his back, with his gun arm beneath him, facing Chimes.

"You aren't going to kill anyone, Chimes. You don't know how to count, you dumb shit! Your gun's empty."

It was that split second that saved Slocum's life. He saw the hesitation in Chimes's face as he reached over and drew his Colt with his left hand. And fired. Chimes's last bullet went through the window of Parker Tilbury's Ajax Feed and Hardware, injuring no one. Slocum's bullet went into Hendry Chimes's guts and killed him.

* * *

"Funny why he took his brother's name," Colonel Humboldt Smithers said later as he patched up a number of cuts and abrasions that Slocum had collected.

"It didn't do much good, anyways," Slocum said. "He is just as dead as his big brother."

The cattle had finally been rounded up hours later by the Klanghorn cowboys, though there were still some strays. The damage to the town had not been small. J. C. Klanghorn had not yet received his final bullet, as Slocum had thought. Hendry Chimes's aim hadn't been any better with the Texan than it had with himself; but the cattleman had been hit in his leg. A number of others had taken lead, and so the Colonel had been called in to help, Doc Herbert Fillmore being overloaded.

"So it was Deal dealing," the Colonel finally said. "Like we thought. I mean, nobody said it, but it was there, am I right?"

"Sure are." Slocum grinned. "I reckon I'll be looking for him."

"And then?"

"Then I got some unfinished business."

The Colonel's big eyeballs were shining. He was delighted. "I got a notion who she is, but I am not saying."

Slocum stood up and looked around the newspaper office. The clutter seemed as bad as it was out in the street.

"You'll arrest Deal, will you?" Humboldt asked.

"On what charges?"

The Colonel pursed his lips and shrugged. "Yeah . . ."

"The man is free. Nobody can prove anything. It's all guess."

"Surmise," said the Colonel, obviously liking the word.

"But you'll be printing the story about Cherokee."

"That I surely will. The frightening, terrorizing Cherokee Bill Hagstrom is finally dead; and peace can come again to our fair land!" The Colonel's forefinger whipped the words into the air as he danced a little jig.

"Except—" He stopped suddenly.

"Except what?" Slocum asked.

"You don't believe that man is dead any more than I do, Slocum!"

"That's right."

"But you want me to print the story so's he'll—"

Colonel Humboldt Smithers never finished his sentence, because at that instant the door of his office burst open and a man burst in.

"Colonel! Ed Deal's been found shot dead and trampled under by them stampeding longhorns. In back of his bank!"

The mordant humor that revealed itself in the death of the town's only undertaker was not lost on Humboldt Smithers, as in his editorial he questioned who would replace this man who had always buried the dead of Horse Creek, Wyoming. Dr. Herbert Fillmore had filled the function for the present at any rate and had even said a few words on behalf of the deceased at graveside. It had been supposed that Ed Deal had died as a result of accident rather than design. A stray bullet, the stampeding cattle. Slocum thought otherwise. For it had been noted that the mayor had been gripping an unfired Smith & Wesson in his hand as he lay dead. Target practice hadn't helped him at all, Slocum reflected sardonically.

He attended the funeral, standing across the grave from Godiva, whose face was wet with tears. Afterward she had approached him with a soft, secret smile, asking if he would care to join her for dinner. Slocum begged off. He knew what she had in mind; not only sex, which would have been fine with him, but surely she needed someone to take Deal's place in the plan, which he was certain the banker had shared with her.

He much preferred to have supper with Kelly Kenton, which he was soon doing. And not very long afterward he was having her. She was all that he had hoped, and by the time morning came around, neither of them had put in much time sleeping.

"The more I have you, the more I want you," she said as the first morning light touched the window of their bedroom at the Denver House.

"Me too," he said, reaching for her again.

Later she said, "I can feel you're starting to leave."

"I don't want to," he said.

"I know. But—well . . ."

"There's still some unfinished business."

She reached down and began teasing his balls, while her tongue played along his lips. "There's unfinished business here," she said.

Slocum said nothing to that. He was too busy to speak.

"How you going to find him?" the Colonel asked. "He's got a start on ya."

"I don't have to find him," Slocum said. "He will find me."

Humboldt's mouth dropped open. "You figger he knows you know he ain't dead."

"No, I don't know what he figgers. Excepting, if I was him, I'd be figuring to make real sure. So I'd be cutting this lawman's trail."

"Gotcha!" Humboldt was working his jaws quickly, like a prairie dog. "He is a funny man, that Cherokee. I mean, getting mad at everybody for just pretending they were himself. I mean, that is something."

"A man lives like Cherokee, he has got to believe he is something," Slocum said. "That is all a man like that has got. It's why he'll be looking to kill me."

"You figure he is still in town?"

"Nearby, I'd—uh—surmise, Colonel." And Slocum gave a wink with it.

Humboldt broke up in laughter, coughing, hawking, spitting, and scratching with delight at the way Slocum had imitated him with his favorite word.

That evening after having supper with Kelly, he took her again to his room in the Denver House.

When they walked into the bedroom, she said, "Is something wrong? You seem . . . different."

"Yes. I am. I want you to go home."

"Oh . . ."

He smiled gently at her, slipping his arm around her waist. "No, I'm not sending you packing. I told you I had some unfinished business, and I see that somebody else has been reminding me of it."

"What do you mean?"

"Someone's been in this room."

"Someone?"

"Someone who wants to tell me he's going to kill me. Someone with a very strange sense of humor. He wants me to be worrying about it."

"Oh, John, you mustn't stay here!"

"I want you to go home. In fact, I'm going to walk you back."

She didn't argue. He walked her back downstairs, out the front door, and down the street, all the way to her cabin.

When they had reached her door, she turned to him and said, "Soon? I know you'll be going away, but couldn't we . . . just one more time?"

"More than one more," he promised. And he left her.

The street was noisy when he walked back to the Denver House. The cowboys were celebrating to their last cent. The girls were obliging, the whiskey and beer flowed freely, and the cards and dice games were thriving.

Slocum walked in the center of the street, keeping clear of the alleys, watching along the rooftops. Luckily it was a moonlit night and he could see a lot.

Suddenly he heard the horses. And in the next moment they burst into sight, coming in from the north, their shadowy figures still clearly outlined in the moonlight. Somebody was hazing them, for he could hear the wrangler's voice. They were almost on him before he could get out of the street.

At first he thought they had to be mustangs, for they were without riders or any rigging, but then he realized they were shod. Some damn fool—drunk, likely—was wrangling a remuda through the middle of town. There must have been twenty of them. Hell, at this time of night! In the next second he thought of the cattle stampede down the same street and he realized what it was. He was almost too late as he dropped to the ground one split second before the bullet whistled past his head. And he heard the furious cry: "Slocum!"

Then he was rolling into an alley next to one of the saloons. But the rider had spotted him, and now horse and rider were bearing down.

Suddenly the door of the saloon burst open and the light thrown into the street illuminated the horse and rider. Slocum, risen to one knee, in the act of drawing his six-gun, saw the big man with the big nose and wiry black beard.

Cherokee Bill's next shot went wild.

Slocum's did not.

They played together for a long time before he mounted her, slipping his rigid organ up high and as deep as it would go into her. She was almost crying from the joy of it. Slowly he began to move his hips while she joined him, bracing her feet on the bed sheets, while he took one springy breast in his mouth and sucked.

Thus they rode, changing pace every now and again to their mutual delight, until with the utmost delicacy, mixed with absolutely savage desire, they brought each other to the exquisite, totally unbearable climax.

Much later as she lay in his arms, she said, "I've the feeling you've gotten your business done with."

"Yes, I have."

"Then you'll be riding off." There was no sorrow in her voice, only the statement of a fact.

"I'll be riding off," he said, taking her once again into his arms. "But not until we're finished."

JAKE LOGAN

J.D. HARDIN

"THE MOST EXCITING WESTERN WRITER SINCE LOUIS L'AMOUR" —JAKE LOGAN

_0-425-07700-4	CARNIVAL OF DEATH #33	$2.50
_0-425-08013-7	THE WYOMING SPECIAL #35	$2.50
_0-425-07257-6	SAN JUAN SHOOTOUT #37	$2.50
_0-425-07259-2	THE PECOS DOLLARS #38	$2.50
_0-425-07114-6	THE VENGEANCE VALLEY #39	$2.75
_0-425-07386-6	COLORADO SILVER QUEEN #44	$2.50
_0-425-07790-X	THE BUFFALO SOLDIER #45	$2.50
_0-425-07785-3	THE GREAT JEWEL ROBBERY #46	$2.50
_0-425-07789-6	THE COCHISE COUNTY WAR #47	$2.50
_0-425-07974-0	THE COLORADO STING #50	$2.50
_0-425-08088-9	THE CATTLETOWN WAR #52	$2.50
_0-425-08669-0	THE TINCUP RAILROAD WAR #55	$2.50
_0-425-07969-4	CARSON CITY COLT #56	$2.50
_0-425-08743-3	THE LONGEST MANHUNT #59	$2.50
_0-425-08774-3	THE NORTHLAND MARAUDERS #60	$2.50
_0-425-08792-1	BLOOD IN THE BIG HATCHETS #61	$2.50
_0-425-09089-2	THE GENTLEMAN BRAWLER #62	$2.50
_0-425-09112-0	MURDER ON THE RAILS #63	$2.50
_0-425-09300-X	IRON TRAIL TO DEATH #64	$2.50
_0-425-09213-5	THE FORT WORTH CATTLE MYSTERY #65	$2.50
_0-425-09343-3	THE ALAMO TREASURE #66	$2.50
_0-425-09396-4	BREWER'S WAR #67	$2.50
_0-425-09480-4	THE SWINDLER'S TRAIL #68	$2.50
_0-425-09568-1	THE BLACK HILLS SHOWDOWN #69	$2.50
_0-425-09648-3	SAVAGE REVENGE #70	$2.50
_0-425-09713-7	TRAIN RIDE TO HELL #71	$2.50
_0-425-09784-6	THUNDER MOUNTAIN MASSACRE #72	$2.50
_0-425-09895-8	HELL ON THE POWDER RIVER #73	$2.75